STAR OF LIGHT

Titles by Patricia M. St. John
STAR OF LIGHT
TREASURES OF THE SNOW
THE TANGLEWOODS' SECRET
RAINBOW GARDEN
THE SECRET OF THE FOURTH CANDLE
THE MYSTERY OF PHEASANT COTTAGE

For older readers:
NOTHING ELSE MATTERS
THE VICTOR
I NEEDED A NEIGHBOUR

For younger readers:
THE OTHER KITTEN
FRISKA, MY FRIEND

STAR OF LIGHT

PATRICIA STJOHN

Scripture Union
130 City Road, London EC1V 2NJ

© Patricia M. St. John 1953
First published 1953
First paperback edition 1969
New paperback edition 1971
Reprinted 1974, 1977
This edition 1980
Ninth reprint 1990

ISBN 0 85421 883 1

Printed and bound in Great Britain by
Cox & Wyman Ltd, Reading

PART ONE

1

A LITTLE girl came running down the side of the mountain one noon in spring. Gathering her cotton gown round her knees, she skipped as lightly as a lamb on her bare brown feet, leaping over drifts of wild marigold that shone up at her. In the water-meadows below her the plum blossom was out, and from the hill-top above it looked like a sea of white foam along the river-banks. Baby goats gambolled among the flowers, and the storks had begun to build on top of the thatches.

Rahma, who had taken a short cut across the hillside, reached the path with a bound, and went on dancing down it. She was seven years old, small because she seldom had enough to eat. Her step-father and the elder wife disliked her, and sometimes beat her. Her clothes were very ragged, and she worked as hard as the mother of a family might work in England; yet all her troubles could not spoil her joy when a treat occasionally came her way—and today she was to look after the goats alone while her brother went on some mysterious expedition with their mother. Free and alone for two whole hours with no other company but the storks and the goats—two whole hours to play in the sunshine with the kids, and no one would scold her, or make her grind the millstone, or carry heavy buckets of water.

She spied her brother from afar, rounding up a couple of mischievous black kids who were trying to get into a patch of young wheat. Spring was making them feel all excited and they gambolled in every direction except the right one, giving merry little bleats and skipping high in the air. Hamid, their keeper, did not mind at all, for he felt exactly as they did. At the margin of the field of young wheat the three of them pranced together, and Rahma came bounding in among them, her smooth dark hair blown in wisps about her face, her black eyes very bright.

Laughing and shouting together they steered the kids on to the open hillside where the rest of the flock was scattered. Then Hamid turned, surprised, to look at his happy little sister. He had not often seen her so gay and abandoned, for country girls are taught to walk sedately and to listen to their elders and betters. Besides, Rahma was seven years old, and almost a little woman.

" What have you come for?" he asked.

" To look after the goats—Mother wants you."

" Why?"

" I don't know—she wants you to go somewhere. She has been crying and looking at little sister. I think perhaps little sister is ill."

Her sparkling eyes clouded as she remembered her mother's tears, for she loved her mother—only the sunshine and freedom had made her forget all about them. Besides, her mother often wept when no one but Rahma was with her, so Rahma was almost used to it.

" All right," said Hamid, " but take good care of the goats; here's a stick for you," and he turned away and climbed the valley between the two green arms of the mountains. He walked fast because he did not want to keep his mother waiting, but he did not skip or look about him as Rahma had done, for his mind was full of wondering.

Why did his mother look so worried these days, as though she were carrying some secret load of fear? And why was she always hiding away his baby sister, keeping her out of sight whenever she heard her husband or the older wife approaching? Of course, neither of them had ever particularly liked baby sister, but they knew she was there, so why hide her? Mother even seemed afraid of him and Rahma playing with their baby nowadays—

she would drive them away, and retreat into a corner of the room, her little daughter clasped against her, and always that fear in her eyes—was it evil spirits she feared? or poison? Hamid did not know, but perhaps today his mother would tell him. He walked faster.

He sighed as he climbed the hill, because until a few months ago his mother had never looked frightened, and he and Rahma had never been knocked about or considered in the way. They had lived with their mother and with their own father, who loved them, in a little thatched home down the valley; there had been three other brown tousled-headed children younger than Rahma, but they had started coughing and grown thin. When the snow fell, and fuel and bread were scarce, they grew weaker and died within a few weeks of each other. Their little bodies were buried on the eastern slope of the mountain facing the sunshine, and marigolds and daisies sprang up on their graves.

Their father coughed that winter too, but no one took any notice, because after all a man must earn his living; so he went on working, and ploughed his spring fields, and sowed his grain. Then he came home one night and said he could work no more. Until the following Autumn he lay on the rush mat and grew weaker. Zohra, his wife, and Hamid and Rahma gathered in the ripened corn, and gleaned what they could in order to buy him food, but it was no use. Then he died, leaving his wife, still young and beautiful, a penniless widow with two little children.

They sold the house and the goat and the hens and the patch of corn, and went to live with the grandmother, until, a few months later, little sister was born, bringing fresh hope and sunshine to the family. They called her Kinza, which means 'treasure,' and never was a baby more loved or fondled; yet, strange to say, she never played or clapped her hands like other babies. She slept a great deal, and often seemed to lie staring at nothing. Hamid sometimes wondered why the bunches of bright flowers he picked for her seemed to give her no pleasure.

When Kinza was a few months old there came a fresh offer of marriage for their mother, and she accepted at once, because she had no work and no more money to buy bread for her two children; and the family moved to their new home.

It was not a very happy home. Si Mohamed, the husband, was already married to an older wife, but she had never had any children, so he wanted another. He did not mind taking Hamid too, because a boy of nine would be useful in looking after the goats; nor did he object to Rahma, because a girl of seven can be a useful little slave about the house; but he could not see that a baby was the slightest use to any of them, and wished to give Kinza away.

" Many childless women will be glad of a girl," he said; " and why should I bring up another man's baby!"

But young Zohra had burst into a passion of weeping and refused to do any work until he changed his mind, so he rather sullenly agreed to let Kinza stay for a time. No more was said about it—unless perhaps something had been said during the past few weeks, something that Hamid and Rahma had not heard; could that be why their mother held Kinza so close, and looked so frightened?

A voice above him called to him to run, and he looked up. His mother was standing under an old twisted olive tree that flung its shade over a well. She carried two buckets in her hand, but she had not filled them, and baby Kinza was tied on her back with a cloth. She seemed in a great hurry about something.

" Come quick, Hamid," she said impatiently. " How slowly you came up the path! Hide the buckets in the bushes—I only brought them as an excuse to leave the house, lest Fatima should want to know why I was going. Now, come with me."

" Where to, Mother?" asked the little boy, very surprised.

" Wait till we get round the corner of the mountain," replied his mother, leading the way up the steep, green grass, and walking very fast. " People will see us from the well, and will tell Fatima where we have gone. Follow quickly. I'll soon tell you."

They hurried on until they had turned the corner of the arm of the mountain and were hidden from the village, and were overlooking another valley. The young mother sat down, unhitched her cloth, and laid her baby in her lap.

"Look well at her, Hamid," she said. "Play with her and show her the flowers."

Hamid, wondering, stared long and earnestly into the strangely old, patient face of his little sister, but she did not stare back or return his smile. She seemed to be looking at something very far away, and not to see him at all. With a sudden thrill of fear he flicked his hand in front of her eyes but she neither moved nor blinked.

"She's blind," he whispered at last. His lips felt dry, and his face was rather white.

His mother nodded, and rose quickly to her feet. "Yes," she replied, "she's blind. I've known it for some time, but I've kept it from Fatima and my husband because when they know they will probably take her away from me—why should they be bothered with another man's blind child? She can never work, and she will never marry . . ."

Her voice broke, and, blinded by her tears, she stumbled a little on the rough track. Hamid caught her arm.

"Where are we going, Mother?" he inquired again.

"To the Saint's tomb," answered his mother, hurrying on, "up behind the next hill. They say he is a very powerful saint and has healed many, but Fatima has never before given me the chance to go. Now she thinks I'm drawing water, and we must return with the buckets full. I wanted you to come with me, because it's a lonely path and I was afraid to go by myself."

They climbed in silence, too breathless to talk any more, until the green, flower-starred turf gave place to rock. Here, hollowed from a boulder, was a small cave shaded by a bush. The bush was festooned with dirty little screws of paper tied to its branches, and every little screw carried its tale of sorrow; the sick, the broken-hearted, the childless, the unloved, all brought their burdens to the bones of this dead man, and they all went home unhealed and uncomforted.

They laid little sister at the mouth of the cave, and the mother bowed down and lifted herself up again, calling on the name of a God about Whom she knew nothing, and on the prophet Mohamet. It was her last hope. But as she prayed a cloud passed across the sun, and a cold shadow fell on the baby. She shivered and began to cry, and groped for her mother's arms. The woman gazed eagerly into her daughter's face for a moment, and then picked her up with a disappointed sigh. God had not listened, for Kinza was still blind.

Hamid rose from where he had been squatting, and he and his mother almost ran down the hill. They were late, and already the sun was setting behind the mountains. The storks flew past with their rattling cry, black against the sky, and Hamid, rebellious and bitterly disappointed, scowled into the sunset—what was the good of it? Little sister would never see it; God apparently did not care, and the dead saint would do nothing to help. Perhaps baby girls were beneath his notice.

They reached the well in silence, and Hamid drew the water for his mother, gave her the buckets, and dashed off down the valley to collect Rahma and the goats. He met them half way up the hill, for Rahma was afraid of the lengthening shadows and wanted to go home. She slipped her small hand into his, and the goats, who also wanted to go home, huddled against their legs.

"Where did you go?" asked Rahma.

"To the saint's tomb," answered Hamid. "Rahma, little sister is blind. Her eyes see nothing but darkness—that's why Mother hides her away. She does not want Fatima and Si Mohamed to know."

Rahma stood still, horrified. "Blind?" she echoed—and then, as the thought struck her, she added quickly, "and the saint—couldn't he make her see?"

Hamid shook his head. "I don't think that saint is much

good," he said rather boldly. "Mother went there before when Father coughed, but nothing happened—Father died."

"It is the will of God," said Rahma, and shrugged her shoulders. Then, clinging close together, because night was falling, they climbed the hill, and the goats' eyes gleamed like green lanterns in the dark.

"I hate the dark," whispered Rahma with a little shiver. But Hamid stared up into the sky, deep blue through a filigree of olive leaves.

"I love the stars," he said.

2

They reached the village ten minutes later, and passed by the dark huts. Through open doors glowing charcoal gleamed cheerfully in clay pots, and families squatted round their evening meal by dim lamp-light. But at some little distance from their own house they could hear the angry voice of Fatima, the older wife, scolding their mother.

Fatima hated the new wife and her three children, and made life as hard as she could for them in every possible way. She was bowed and withered by long years of drudgery, and Zohra was still young and beautiful. Fatima had longed in vain for a baby, while Zohra had had six, so perhaps it was small wonder that the older woman was so jealous, and had been so angry at their coming. She vented her hatred by sitting cross-legged on the mattress like a queen all day, and making Zohra and Rahma work like slaves. Zohra had only escaped to the well because Fatima had fallen asleep—and unfortunately she had not slept long. Furious at the young woman's absence, she had sent a neighbouring child to the top of the hill to spy out her whereabouts—so Zohra, carrying her buckets, had arrived home to find that Fatima knew all about her expedition.

"Wicked, deceitful, lazy one!" shouted Fatima. "You can't deceive me. Give me that child! let me see for myself why you hide her away, and hold her so secretly, and creep with her to the tomb—give me her, I say. I insist on having her."

She snatched the baby roughly from Zohra's grasp, and carried her to the light, and the mother with a resigned gesture of despair let her empty arms fall to her side. After all, Fatima must know soon. They could not hide it much longer, and she had better find out for herself.

The frightened children squatted in the shadows by the wall, their dark eyes very big. The hut was silent as Fatima passed her hands over the baby limbs, and stared into Kinza's still face. Hamid, holding his breath, was conscious of little sounds he had never noticed before—the slow, rhythmical munching of the ox in the stall; the rustle of straw as the kids nuzzled against their mothers; and the subdued crooning of roosted hens.

Then the silence was broken by a triumphant cackle of laughter from the old woman, and Kinza, whose ears were acutely sensitive to loud noises and angry voices, gave a frightened cry. Fatima picked her up and almost flung her back into her mother's lap.

"Blind," she announced—"blind as night!—and you knew—you knew all the time! You brought her here to your husband's house to be a burden on us all for ever—never to work, never to marry—and you hid her away lest we should know. Oh, most deceitful of women! Our husband shall know about this tonight. Now up and prepare his supper, and you, Rahma, blow up the charcoal. When he has eaten his food we shall hear what he has to say."

The frightened little girl sprang up and set to work with the bellows till the flames leaped from the glowing charcoal and flung strange shadows on the walls. Zohra, trembling, laid her baby in the swinging wooden cradle that hung from a beam, and set to work to mash the beans and beat in the oil, for her husband had gone to speak to a neighbour, and would be in any time now. They were only just ready when they heard his firm steps coming along the path, and a moment later he appeared in the doorway, a tall man, black-eyed and black-bearded, with a hard, cruel mouth. He wore a long garment of dark homespun goat's wool, with a white turban wound round his head. He did not speak to his wives or to his step-children, but sat down cross-legged in front of the low, round table and motioned for the food to be set before him. If he noticed Fatima's triumph, and the white, scared faces of Zohra and the children, he said nothing.

Zohra set the hot dish in the centre of the table and the silent family gathered round. There were no spoons, but she broke two large pieces of bread for her husband and Fatima and three small pieces for herself, Hamid, and Rahma.

"In the name of God," they murmured as they scooped their bread in the centre dish, for the words would drive away evil spirits who might be lurking round the table. Sometimes at midday when the sun was shining Rahma forgot to say them, but she never forgot at night, for the flickering shadows and dark corners made her feel afraid; evil spirits seemed very real and near after the lamps had been lit. And certainly tonight the little home was full of evil spirits—dark spirits of jealousy and anger and hatred and cruelty and fear. Even little Kinza in her hanging cradle seemed to feel the atmosphere, and wailed fretfully. Si Mohamed frowned.

"Stop that noise," he growled. "Pick her up."

The mother obeyed, and sat down again with her baby held very close against her breast. Fatima waited a moment until her husband had finished eating, then she held out her arms.

"Give that child to me," she said threateningly, and Zohra handed over her baby and burst into tears.

"What is the matter?" asked Si Mohamed irritably. His wives might quarrel all they pleased—wives always did quarrel—but he disliked them doing it in front of him. He had been ploughing all day, and was tired.

"Yes, what is the matter indeed!" sneered Fatima, and she held out the baby at arm's length so that the lamp-light suddenly shone straight on to her face. But she neither screwed up her eyes nor turned from it. Si Mohamed stared at her fixedly.

"Blind!" cried Fatima, as she had shouted before. "Blind, blind, blind! and Zohra knew it—she has deceived us all."

" I didn't," sobbed Zohra, rocking to and fro.

" You did," shouted the old woman.

" Silence, you women," said their husband sternly, and the quarrel ceased instantly. Once again there was silence in the dim hut. Rahma suddenly felt cold with fear, and crept closer to the dying charcoal. Her step-father scrutinized the tiny face—flashed the light in front of it—jerked his hands towards it, until he was satisfied that the old woman spoke the truth.

" Truly," he agreed, " she is blind."

But the dreaded outburst of rage never came. He handed Kinza back to her mother, half closed his eyes, and lit a long thin pipe. He sat puffing away in silence for some time, until the hut was filled with sickly fumes, and then he said,

" Blind children can be very profitable—keep that baby carefully. She may bring us much money."

" How?" asked Zohra nervously, her arms tightening on her baby.

" By begging," replied her husband. " Of course, we cannot take her begging ourselves, for I am a very honourable man; but there are beggars who would be glad to hire her to sit with them in the markets; people are sorry for blind children, and give liberally I believe I know of one who would pay to borrow her when she is a little older."

Zohra said nothing—she dared not; but Hamid and Rahma gave each other a long rebellious look across the table. They knew the beggar of whom their father spoke —an old man dressed in filthy, ancient rags, who swore horrible oaths. They did not want their precious Kinza to go to that old man. He would certainly ill-treat her and frighten her.

Their father saw the look through half-closed eyelids. He clapped his hands sharply.

" To bed, you children," he ordered, " quick!"

They rose hurriedly, mumbled goodnight, and scuttled into dark corners of the room. There were low mattresses laid along the wall; curling themselves up on these, they pulled strips of blanket over them, and fell fast asleep.

Hamid never knew why he woke that night, for he usually slept soundly till sunrise; but about two in the morning he suddenly sat up in bed, wide awake. A patch of bright moonlight was shining through the window on to Kinza's cradle, and she was moaning and stirring in her sleep.

Hamid slipped from his mattress, and stood beside her. Suddenly a great wave of protective tenderness seemed to come sweeping over him. She was so small, so patient, and so defenceless. Well, he would see to it that no harm came to her. All his life he would guide her through her darkness, and protect her with his love. His heart swelled for a moment, and then he remembered that he was only a boy himself and completely in his step-father's hand. They might take Kinza away from him, and then his love would be powerless to reach her.

Was there no stronger love to shelter her, no more certain light to lead her? He did not know.

3

BLIND Kinza sat in the doorway of her hut and lifted her small face to the sunshine. It was Thursday, and on Thursday Kinza went to work. She was two-and-a-half years old now, and quite old enough, in her father's opinion, to earn her living like the rest of them.

She sat still and patient, her weak legs folded under her, her hands clasped quietly in her lap. It was quite early, and Hamid, who carried her to her job, had taken the cow to pasture and would not be back for half an hour or so. In the meantime she was free to enjoy herself, and Kinza enjoyed herself quite a lot in her own way.

As long as the sun shone and the weather was fine she was, on the whole, a happy little child. Never having seen the light she could not miss it, and there were many good things to feel. There was the warmth and shelter of her mother's lap, the clasp of her brother's strong arms, and the wet noses of kids nuzzled into her hands. There was the touch of the sun on her body and the wind on her face. Sometimes she was allowed to sit by her mother as she sorted the corn, and Kinza would pick up handfuls of worn husks and let them slip through her fingers. That was one of her greatest treats.

There were lovely things to hear, too, and she knew now that Hamid was coming towards her, from the particular sound of his bare feet on the dry mud. She held up her arms and gave a delighted squeak. Hamid picked her up and tied her firmly on his back.

"Market day, little sister," he announced. "Have you had some breakfast?"

Kinza nodded. Half an hour ago she had drunk a bowlful of sweet black coffee and eaten a hunk of brown bread. It was the best breakfast she knew, and she had enjoyed it immensely.

"Come then," said Hamid, and they set off together, keeping under the olives to begin with, because by nine o'clock in the summer the sun was blazing hot. But very soon they left the olive trees behind them, and the path to market ran between wheat-fields ripe for harvest; every stalk was bowed with heavy gold, and the air was drowsy with the smell of poppies. Kinza, who could go to sleep whenever and wherever she pleased, laid her head down on her brother's shoulder and shut her eyes, lulled by the sound of the wind rustling over the corn.

There were many people on the path that morning, for on Thursday, instead of the village going to the market, the market came to the village. Each of the larger villages had its own special day when all who had anything to sell travelled over the mountains and squatted on their particular marketplace—which is why the name of Hamid's village meant Thursday. Several times on their journey Hamid backed into the corn to make way for some stately merchant riding along on horseback, with his wife, bowed down under some heavy burden, panting along behind him.

As they reached the market-place the crowds became thicker. It was an area of burnt yellow grass, shaded by eucalyptus trees, and the sellers sat cross-legged on the ground, with their wares piled up in front of them, while the buyers stampeded round them. Kinza hated it. She hated the jostling and jolting and noise, she hated the dust that made her sneeze, and the flies that crawled over her face, and the fleas that bit her legs. Most of all she hated the moment when Hamid deserted her and left her to the care of the old beggar.

But Hamid, in order to ease the pain of parting, had contrived a plan. If during the week he could beg, borrow, or steal a gourda (a coin worth less than a tenth of a penny), he would save it until Thursday morning, and as they crossed the market he would exchange it proudly for a lump of sticky green candy, studded with nuts. And licking that green candy was the biggest treat Kinza knew.

Hamid, very much at home in the market, steered his way deftly through the crowds, elbowing, ducking, and dodging until he reached the patch of sand where Kinza and the old beggar sat side by side. He made a point of arriving before the beggar because that gave him time to settle Kinza on the sand to eat the green candy. Hamid took a few secret licks himself first, and then handed it over, warm and wet, to his sister. She clasped it in her right hand, loving its sweet stickiness, and began to lick it all over, going round and round with the tip of her little pink tongue. In her left hand she clutched the hem of Hamid's tunic tightly, lest the roaring crowd should sweep him away from her.

They had not been there long before the old beggar came shuffling towards them, with a coloured drum in his hand. He was amazingly dirty and old, and his coat looked like a patchwork quilt falling to pieces. Hamid kissed his hand politely and received the coin that was paid to his father weekly for the loan of Kinza. But, instead of dismissing him curtly as he usually did, the old beggar spoke to him.

"When your father comes down to buy," he growled, "tell him I have business with him."

Hamid nodded, freed himself gently from Kinza's grasp, and made off; and Kinza, finding herself bereft, wept a little, until the old beggar noticed and slapped her for it.

Her work was not very difficult during the early part of the day. All she had to do was to sit with her small face lifted to the light so that all could see she was blind, and hold out her hand. The old beggar sat beside her, thumping his drum to make people look at her, and chanting and swaying. Quite a number felt sorry for the tiny white-faced child, and gave her coins which she handed to her master. So they sat until noon, and the sun rose higher, and the dust and the flies grew thicker. The crowd milled round them and the stray dogs sniffed them. Once or twice somebody failed to see her at all, and tripped right over her.

At noon Kinza's master gave her a piece of dark rye-bread and a cup of water, and because she had collected quite a lot of money during the morning he gave her a squashed plum. It was delicious. She sucked all her ten fingers in turn, lest she should lose one drop of the juice.

The afternoon was harder than the morning, for by two o'clock Kinza began to grow sleepy. Her dark head, tied up in its cotton cloth, began to nod heavily, and her eyes just would not keep open. She longed for her mother's lap, so all unnoticed she nestled against the old man's rags and found a place of rest for her weary head.

But only for a few minutes. He saw what had happened, and jerked her angrily upright. Bewildered, she rubbed her knuckles in her eyes, stretched herself, and tumbled forward. Once again he jerked her back, slapped her, and propped her up against him, and thus with her outstretched hand supported by the other she sat begging, half-asleep, dreaming no doubt of beautiful baby secrets, until the beggar suddenly got up in a hurry and she fell over sideways.

He sat her up with an impatient bump. " Bad child!" he growled, " sit and beg till I come back."

He had risen because, on the outskirts of the crowd, he had seen the tall figure of Kinza's step-father looking about for him. The farmer would not wish to speak to the beggar in the open market, so they withdrew together behind a huge eucalyptus tree and stood talking.

" You wanted me?" asked the farmer.

" Yes," said the old beggar. " I'm leaving the village. The country people are growing greedy and irreligious, and give little to honourable beggars, so I'm going to the great town on the coast—I and my wife. The great feast will soon be here, and they say beggars grow rich in the streets of the town. Now this is what I want to say—Give me that blind child of yours. You are not one of the noble profession of beggars, and you can never make use of her, but she brings me great gain. My wife will look after her, and I will pay you a good sum for her."

Kinza's step-father hesitated. He knew that he was plotting a very wicked thing, but he needed money badly. His cow had strayed into a neighbour's corn and had been put in the cows' prison. It could only be redeemed at a high price. His harvest was poor this year, and Kinza, while she earned little, was and always would be an extra mouth to feed.

Some faint feeling that might once have been a conscience stirred in him, but he refused to listen to it. After all, Kinza was not his child. Hamid was eleven, almost a man, and could soon be turned adrift to earn his own living, and Rahma could be married off in three or four years. But this might be the first and last chance he would ever have of getting rid of Kinza.

"How much will you give me?" he said at last.

The beggar mentioned a small sum. The farmer fell into a towering rage at such meanness, and mentioned a very large sum. The beggar fell into a towering rage at such covetousness, but stated his price a little higher, while the farmer consented to come a little lower. Thus the bargaining went on. You would have thought they were about to murder each other, but the passers-by hardly turned their heads. For that is the way prices are fixed in the country, and the final sum was exactly half-way between what both had asked in the first place.

"Right," said the beggar at last. "I'll be leaving the village at dawn on the first day of the week. When you hand over the child I will hand over the money, and it shall be done in the presence of witnesses."

Though neither showed it, both were pleased. The old beggar fought his way back to his newly-purchased property, hoping she had managed to collect some coins during his absence. But his newly-purchased property had done nothing of the sort. She had crept into a patch of dappled sun and shade and lay fast asleep, curled up in a ball like a tired kitten.

4

HAMID stood on the outskirts of the market, his thin brown face upturned, and his eyes glued to the top of the mosque, waiting for the priest to appear and shout the four o'clock prayer-call. That call sounded the hour of Kinza's release, when he might carry her off, safe for another week.

The crowd was thinning now, and Hamid caught occasional glimpses of his sister sitting in a dejected little heap beside her master. She was in disgrace from having fallen asleep, and her weary attitude made Hamid impatient to rescue her. He stood first on one bare foot and then on the other. Then he stood on both and wriggled his toes in the hot sand, but he never moved his bright, dark eyes from the top of the mosque.

The mosque was the village temple—a building with a square tower dazzling white against the burning blue. From its summit rose a gleaming golden crescent, and, as Hamid stood watching, the old priest appeared, bearded and majestic in his robes of office, and sent his chanted prayer-call ringing across the market to the village beyond:

" There is one God," he cried, "and Mahomet is his prophet." Faithful Moslems flocked to the temple to recite their prayer. Others took off their shoes and prayed where they stood, facing east, bowing low, and sometimes kneeling with their foreheads on the ground. To them it was a prayer-call, but to Hamid it was the call of Kinza's release. The instant he caught sight of the priest he scudded across the market, kissed the old beggar's hand in greeting, and snatched up his little sister.

He had brought her a leathery ring of fried dough; she clutched it eagerly and took a mouthful. In the joy of feeling his arms safe about her once more she forgot all the hunger and thirst and weariness of that long day, and nestled her downy head into his neck, crooning with delight. Her tired muscles and stiff back relaxed; she dribbled as she ate her mouthful of doughnut, tucked the rest of it down her dress, and went fast asleep, as she had been longing to do for the past three hours. Hamid, a little bowed by the dead weight of her, wandered home along the river-path in the sweltering heat.

It was so hot that he sat down to rest under a fig-tree and watched the lazy cows in the shallows of the river. A few women were washing their clothes just above where the cows stood, rubbing their white garments on stones. Half drowsily he began thinking about the river. Where did it go when it left his valley and flowed out into a strange world where he had never been? One day he would go and see—he would go when the oleanders were out, and follow their pink, winding tracks all the way to the great ocean.

Once again, as night fell, the family gathered round the clay bowl and ate their supper by firelight and candlelight. Kinza woke up, refreshed by her sleep, and sat on her mother's knees, flushed and bright-eyed, opening her mouth for food like a hungry baby bird. Hamid watched her, loving her, and remembering the pressure of her weary little body against his back—always, always, he would protect her and make her happy.

The cows munched in the shed, and an old dog with a torn ear wandered in and lay down with his head on Rahma's lap. Moths and bats fluttered in and out, and the cat crept up and stuck her head into the clay pot to have supper with the family. Twice they pushed her away, but she was very persistent so in the end they let her be. After all, there was plenty for everyone.

A tiny wind breathed into the doorway, sweet with the smell of herbs which grew in boxes outside the hut. Hamid, tired by his climb, lay down to sleep, and in his dreams the old beggar seemed to get bigger and bigger, till somehow he stood, enormous and terrifying, between him and

Kinza . . . He woke suddenly to find that the moon had risen and the grown-ups were still sitting talking round the dead charcoal.

It must have been some new quality of fear or urgency in his mother's voice that woke him, for they were not talking loudly. In the silver beams he could see their faces clearly—his father grim and determined, Fatima cruelly pleased, his mother pale and pleading.

"It is the only offer we shall ever get for her," said Si Mohamed doggedly. "She will be provided for for life."

"Life!" cried the mother bitterly, "there will be no life! She will die—she is so little and so weak. . . ."

"A blind child is better dead!" remarked Fatima.

The mother turned angrily on the old woman, but the father silenced them both by raising his hand.

"Silence, you foolish women!" he ordered. "Let there be no more talk about this. The child must come with me three days from now at dawn."

He rose majestically, and Fatima rose too; but Zohra stayed crouched by the dead fire, rocking herself to and fro in the moonlight.

"Little daughter! little daughter!" she murmured brokenly to herself, and Hamid lay quite still and watched her. He dared not speak or go to her for fear of waking his step-father. But his hot little heart beat very fast, and his mind was resolutely made up.

"It shall not be!" he said to himself over and over again. "I will not let her go. It shall not be!"

He watched his mother creep away from the embers at last and lie down sorrowfully to sleep. He watched the patch of moonlight move across the doorway and encircle the cradle where Kinza lay dreaming. He saw the pale summer dawn begin to glimmer, and heard the first cock-crow and the cattle turn over in the stall—all the time he lay thinking, thinking, thinking. But his thinking got him nowhere, and just before daybreak he fell into a deep sleep; to be woken two hours later by his step-father prodding him with his foot.

"Wake up, you lazy creature!" growled Si Mohamed. "It's time you had the goats out."

Hamid rolled off his mattress, washed his face and hands in a bucket, and started to eat his breakfast. Gobbling his bread and sipping his bowl of coffee he glanced at his mother. Her face was pale, and there were dark circles under her eyes, but she did not look as unhappy as he had expected. There was a very determined expression in her face, as though she had quite made up her mind about something. Once Hamid found her staring hard at him, and he returned her gaze, steady and equally determined. She raised her eyebrows a little and he gave a slight nod. A secret understanding flashed between them. At the earliest possible opportunity they would hold council together.

They did not have to wait very long. Hamid drove out his goats and left them browsing on the hillside, well out of sight behind the prickly pear hedges. With a crust of bread saved from his breakfast he bribed a friend to keep an eye on them, and then crept back and watched through a gap in the hedge. Presently he saw his mother go across to the barn where the grindstone stood, and after a few minutes he slipped in and joined her.

Kinza was sitting as usual with her face lifted to the eastern mountain, for any moment now the sun would rise over the top of it. Hamid's mother sat cross-legged, turning the heavy wheel, and the granary smelt sweet with the fragrance of crushed corn. Hamid crouched down beside her and laid his hand on her arm.

"Mother," he whispered, "I heard last night. Is it the old beggar who is having Kinza?"

His mother turned towards him, and her calm steady gaze rested on him for a moment, as though weighing him up. He was a thin little boy, small for his age, but tough and wiry—and his love for Kinza was very strong.

"So my husband thinks," she replied, "but I say that

it shall not be. I will not have Kinzá starved in those cruel streets. No, Hamid, you must take her somewhere else—you can save her if you wish."

"Me!" echoed Hamid, amazed: but the look he turned on his mother was reassuring. It was full of gallant, willing courage—and there was just a trace of merriment in it, too.

5

"LISTEN," said his mother. She turned from the grind-stone, and laid her hands on his knees. In the cool half-light of the granary her voice sounded strangely impressive to Hamid—like words burned into his very soul. His eyes never left her face as she spoke, and all his life he never forgot what she said to him.

"Four years ago," said the mother, "at the time of the great pilgrimage, your father took me to the tomb across the mountains. We left you children with your grand-mother, but I carried your little brother Absalom on my back, because he was only a baby. After we had visited the tomb, your father wished to go on to the town twenty miles beyond, in order to see the market and trade a little. All day we walked, from sunrise to sunset, and the sun beat down on us, and the lorries bringing the pilgrims back to the main road rattled past, half-choking us with dust. By the time we reached the town my feet were cut and blistered and Absalom was crying and feverish. His eyelids were swollen and stuck together, and he could not look at the light.

"It was a pleasant town, with fountains running in the streets. I bathed Absalom's eyes in the clean cold water. We slept in the inn yard, under the stars, and I felt rested when we woke next morning, but Absalom's eyes were still closed and swollen with the heat and dust. Your father went off to the market, but I sat holding my baby, shading his eyes from the light, and brushing the flies off him, for there were many donkeys in the yard, and the place seemed black with flies. As I sat there, a woman of the town came up and began chatting to me, and as we chatted she noticed the child.

30

" ' Your baby is sick? ' " she asked.

" ' Yes,' I replied, and turned his face towards her so that she might see.

" She got up quickly. 'Come quick,' she said; 'there's just time. I'll take you to the house of the English nurse; she'll give you good medicine and heal your baby. She healed my little boy when he rubbed prickly pear thorns into his eyes.'

" I hung back, 'I have no money,' I said.

" ' It doesn't matter,' replied the woman; 'she is a holy woman, and heals without money for love of her Saint. He is a good Saint and has mercy on the poor.'

" ' But,' I objected, 'the English are rich, and live in grand houses. She will not receive me.'

" ' But she lives in one of our houses,' answered the woman; 'and those who go to her for healing are mostly poor. None are ever turned away—I tell you she receives them in the name of her Saint.'

" So I followed, much afraid, but eager for the medicine that would cure my baby's eyes. She led me down a narrow back street to a house with an open door. There were people coming out of that door—poor people like me, with babies tied on their backs. Some carried bottles of medicine and none of them looked afraid.

" We were only just in time, for the room within was nearly empty, and later on we might not have found the nurse at home. She was tall, and her hair and eyes were light. I had never seen anyone like her before. She spoke graciously to all, and I saw her take little children up in her arms as though she loved them. As I watched her, my fear went away, and when everyone else had gone I went up to her and held out Absalom. She led me to a mattress and we sat down together. She took Absalom in her lap and examined his eyes. Her hands were very gentle. He didn't even cry.

" She asked me many questions about him, and then she gave me medicine for his fever and ointment for his eyes. While she fetched them I looked at a picture on the wall.

It was the picture of a Man with a kind face, holding a little child in his arms, and lots of other little children clinging to his robe, looking up at him.

"I asked her who that Man was, and she said it was one called Jesus, Who was sent from God to show us the way to Heaven. She told me a lot about Him; how He healed the sick, and made blind people see, and loved all men, rich and poor, grown-ups and children. I can't remember all she said, but I know she loved the Man in the picture and wanted to be like Him—and that was why she gave medicine and was kind to Absalom."

Zohra paused, and then went on speaking very slowly.

"And I think for the sake of the Man in the picture she would shelter Kinza, and so you must carry Kinza to her. You must start tonight when the moon is full, and you must walk all night and hide by day—for Si Mohamed will certainly search for you; but he need not know you have gone till tomorrow night. I will send Rahma out early with the goats before he's awake, and tell him you have taken them. He never troubles to look at Kinza, in any case, and I'll put a pillow in the cradle in case Fatima glances in. By the time he comes home from work it will be dusk, and he cannot send out a search by night, nor will I tell him where you've gone. By the next day you will be nearly there."

The child's eyes were bright with fear and excitement, but he only said,

"How shall I know the way?"

"I've thought of that," replied his mother, "and there is only one road on which you can travel. If you take the main bus road you will certainly be seen, and it is the longest way round. The direct way through the mountains is too lonely, and you would never find it. But there is a third way, and that you must take. You must follow the river to the top of the valley and then you must climb the mountain. It is very high, but you must just journey to the top. Below you will see another river in a valley, and if you follow the road along the bank, you will at last reach a big main road with traffic—cars and big lorries laden with tree-trunks from the forests. If you start walking up this road, it may be one of these lorries will give you a ride, for the town lies about 50 kilometres along it up in the mountains. If you cannot get a ride you must walk it, and may God help you."

"And when I get there?" breathed the little boy.

"When you get there," said his mother, "you must find the house of the English nurse. Do not ask, but just watch. She lives in a street behind the market and opposite the doorway of the inn. Her house is the last one in the street. A passage runs up the side of her house. Go to her, tell her all our story, and give her Kinza. She will know what to do next."

Hamid looked doubtful. "But what if she doesn't want Kinza?" he asked.

The mother shook her head. "She won't turn her away," she replied confidently. "She told me her Saint in the picture never turned anyone away. For the sake of her Saint I know she will receive her and be good to her. Now you must go back to your goats, and I must finish the grinding, or Fatima will be so angry. Think on what I've told you, and I'll bake extra loaves of bread for you to carry on your journey."

Hamid rose to go back to his goats, feeling like someone in a dream. The sun had risen over the mountain while they were talking, and Kinza on the step was laughing and stretching out her arms. The goats cropped the pasture, the river sparkled and the harvest fields gleamed. The world was really just the same as it had been yesterday, but to the eyes of the little boy it seemed different. His friends the mountains looked suddenly strange and menacing now that he knew he must cross them alone, and he no longer wanted to know where the river went. Yet in spite of his fear he never thought of refusing to go.

He whistled softly; a few young goats grazing near came up to him pushing their noses into his lap, and he suddenly knew that he loved them, and was sorry to leave them. These were the kids he had taught to walk, and carried when they were tired, and switched when they made for the young corn. He fondled their ears and stumpy horns, and wondered when he would see them again. For the first time he began to consider his own future, as well as Kinza's. He certainly could not come back for a long time. His step-father would be much too angry.

He led them home early that evening and sat quietly down beside his mother and Rahma, who were busy spinning wool. Rahma teasled out the raw tangle on two pin-studded pieces of wood, and his mother turned the fuzzy cones on her wheel, drawing them into threads. Both were working very hard, because Fatima was sitting by watching, and neither spoke when Hamid joined them.

Yet he felt the sympathy of their silent companionship and his young heart ached. Except when his mother had gone on that five days' pilgrimage, he had never spent a night of his life away from her. Now he must leave her for a long time. He dared not speak in the presence of the old woman, but it did not matter. Her silent love flowed out to him, comforting him, strengthening him; Rahma, who knew nothing of what was happening, broke into a happy little chant as she tossed her wool.

The evening dragged on and the light faded. Sunset flamed in the sky, and paled again; dusk fell, and then night. The little boy sat and watched, as he had watched hundreds of times before, but tonight it was different. For the first time in his life he was not hungry when the family gathered round the supper bowl, but he forced himself to eat lest his father should notice. Then without a word he went out and lay down by the door and waited, battling with his fears and thoughts until his father should go to sleep, and the moon should rise.

He watched his father lie down at last, and listened till his breathing became heavy and regular—yes, he was sleeping deeply, snoring in his dreams. Only a little longer now. Hamid crept to the edge of the mattress, and waited with his eyes glued to the mountain. Already the crest was outlined against a circle of light. On silent feet Hamid stepped through the doorway and slipped behind the granary.

The old dog cocked its ears and rattled its chain, and Hamid held his breath. If the dog should bark the whole plan would be ruined. He flung himself down beside it, burying his face in its mangy coat, fondling its ears, and speechlessly imploring it to be silent. It turned its large head and licked the child's cheek, puzzled but loyal.

So he crouched waiting, with his arms round the dog's neck, listening for his mother. The home scents of cattle and crushed corn wafted round him, but the path, a white ribbon in the moonlight, lured him on to his great adventure. He jumped as his mother, with Kinza in her arms, appeared round the granary, noiseless as a ghost.

In complete silence she bound Kinza to his back. The baby bewildered, but perfectly trustful, laid her head down on his shoulder and went fast asleep again. Then his mother tied two loaves of bread on his other shoulder, took both his hands in hers and kissed them. He in turn pressed her fingers to his lips and clung close to her for a moment. Then she put him gently from her and stood watching as he passed out of the gate. Not a word had passed between them. Then, content with what she had done, she went back to her hut—to the empty cradle and the anger of her husband. And Hamid, like some small craft cut loose from its moorings and swept out into uncharted seas, set off along his silver path.

6

THE path did not remain silver for long. It dipped into the black shadows of the olive trees, and Hamid shivered and stumbled over a root. Righting himself, he hurried on, and came out on the open, where the grass was short and burnt. Hamid glanced up at the low pass between the hills and made towards it. Passing straggling groups of huts he reached the top of the hill out of breath, and paused for a last backward look at his home.

He could see it quite clearly—a prickly pear hedge surrounding a mud yard, enclosing all that had been his world up till now; a thatched hut, a charcoal fire and a cradle; mother and the little sister; the spinning wheel, the corn sieve, the water pots and the grindstone; a small fawn cow and a flock of goats; an old dog with torn ears —it had been a very pleasant life as long as the weather was warm and his step-father kept out of the way. Then he went over the top of the pass, and his home was lost to view. Instead, there stretched out at his feet a strange new moonlit world and a silver road winding towards high mountains.

And then as he jogged downhill to the plain he suddenly felt afraid, for he was passing the outskirts of the village burial ground, and surely there must be evil spirits lingering in this place of death. He began to run, but remembered that he was close to those three little graves where some four years ago they had laid Absalom and Mohamed and Habeeba. Their baby spirits, at least, were not evil. He wondered where they were. Hamid did not know. Perhaps that Saint called Jesus, who took little ones in His arms, had mercy on lost children stolen away by death. He murmured the name softly to himself as a talisman against all that might harm him and, still running, reached the path by the river.

Looking back later on, he remembered little about the weary hours of that first night. He arrived at the stony road by the river, and trudged the length of the plain on feet that began to feel sore and bruised. Sometimes an owl hooted from an olive tree and made him jump, but otherwise his eyes were so heavy that he seemed to be walking in a dream. Kinza, slumbering, lay like a dead weight on his back, and seemed to grow much heavier as the night passed. One thing only he noticed clearly, and that was the circling courses of the stars above him. He also noticed that the ground beneath his feet was no longer flat. He had begun climbing.

Half an hour later, still stumbling upwards, he realized that light was stealing over the mountain. Heavy-eyed, white-faced, footsore and cold, he turned to look behind him. He had come a good way through the night, and since his father was unlikely to discover his flight until evening, he was safe to cross the peak that day. On the morrow he must hide from sunrise to sunset.

Soon Kinza woke up. Hamid broke two pieces off the loaf, and they munched in silence. Then he led her to a little stream running down the side of the path, and she drank from his cupped hands. He washed her, too, as well as he could, for it was important that she should look attractive when they reached their unknown friend. He wished he had asked his mother for a quarter of the family comb, so that Kinza could have looked a little less like a neglected doll. He tried dragging his fingers through her matted curls; but Kinza objected to this and slapped him. Being very tired and out of sorts he slapped back, at which Kinza set up a loud roar for her mother and her morning bowl of black coffee. She could not understand what was happening or where she was, and in any case she hated being washed. So for a time they sat together by the stream, sniffing and miserable.

But after a time, having exhausted her rage, Kinza

groped towards him with her arms, nestled into his lap, stuck her thumb in her mouth and forgave him. He looked down at her rather desperately. She was so heavy, and his back ached so, but they must get a little farther before the sun grew really hot. So he hauled her up, and set off again, and the path up the mountain seemed to grow steeper and steeper. There was, however, one comfort. The path climbed along the edge of the runneling brook, and every ten minutes or so he stopped to bathe his feet, or walked a little way among the cold cresses that bordered the water. He passed huts nestling in a hollow on his left and little patches of sloping land where ripe corn rustled. He picked a handful of ears to munch on his journey, and climbed on through rocky olive groves, leaving the stream behind him. Kinza, wide awake and enjoying herself, bounced up and down on his back and pummelled his aching shoulders, and the sun rose higher, burning his head.

He must stop. If he did not lie down somewhere he felt sure that he would fall asleep as he walked. He looked round, but the whole landscape seemed to swim in front of him. Then beyond the shadows of the olive groves he saw a gleam of gold, and knew he was coming to another little patch of harvest.

He never quite remembered how he arrived, and he never even noticed that the field was dangerously near a village. He crept in among the stems, right into the heart of the corn and fell fast, fast asleep. The field, white already to harvest, hid him safely.

Kinza, however, who had slept excellently all night, saw no reason why she should sit in such an uncomfortable spot all day. At home she wandered where she liked, and cornstalks are prickly. Also, Kinza was very hungry. Her mother had never deserted her before, and was sure to be near at hand if only she could escape from this extraordinary place where things tickled her legs and made her sneeze. She uncurled herself resolutely and battled ahead, following that sure instinct of hers to travel towards light. She emerged from the corn patch without much difficulty, and stood listening intently. Then—oh joy!—her keen ears caught the faint humming of a grindstone not far away. Grindstones meant Mother, and Mother meant shelter and food and comfort and security and an end of all strange, rustling, prickly places. With a shrill cry of delight she staggered towards the sound, with outstretched arms.

The woman sitting at the door of her hut heard the cry and looked up. Then she sat staring and staring as though she had seen a ghost, for there lurched toward her on unsteady feet the queerest little figure she had seen in her life; it was a tiny child in a dirty cotton gown, her outstretched hands groping, her face lifted to the light. Her curls, matted into a thick black bush, were crowned with a halo of straw. She was covered all over with wheat chaff, and as the woman sat staring at her the apparition began to sneeze.

So as soon as the noise of grinding ceased, Kinza, no longer guided by the sound, and knowing herself in a strange place, stood irresolute for a moment. Then she held up her arms, and said one word—"Ima!" (Mother).

The woman sitting at the grindstone was a young woman. The previous winter had been a hard one. Her husband's crop had been poor, and the cow had sickened; they had been very hungry and very poor. Her only child had died, and one dark day they had buried him under the snow. So now, when this baby staggered towards her and lisped the very word she had longed to hear for six lonely months, she stopped neither to reason nor to wonder. She drew the dirty little creature into her lap, held it tight, and began crooning over it and kissing it.

Kinza resisted a little at first, and whimpered. She knew that these were the wrong arms, and that this woman was not her mother; but after all they were strong safe arms, and the hand caressing her curls was a gentle hand. Her stiff little body relaxed, and she lay at peace and asked for a drink. Her new friend fetched her a bowl of butter-milk, and Kinza sat up. Holding the bowl in both hands, she drained it to the last drop. Then, looking even odder, because of the white milky rim round her mouth, she curled up kitten-like in the woman's lap and went to sleep.

It was evening when Hamid woke up and lay wondering where he was. He seemed to be lying in shadow looking up at a golden roof, where the sloping rays of light caught the ears of wheat. His body ached, but he felt rested and comfortable. As he lay there it gradually all came back to him; then he sprang up with a little cry of concern.

Where was Kinza?

In spite of his fright he knew he must be cautious, so he crept to the edge of the patch. He could see her tracks, because the wheat was broken and the poppies were crushed. They had come in on the lower side; she had gone out on the upper side, and he peered through the stalks in the direction she must have taken. What he saw was a great surprise.

Not fifty yards from where he crouched stood a hut, and on the step, perfectly at home, and apparently not missing him in the least, sat Kinza, eating cherries. Her foster-mother sat behind her in the doorway, laughing and trying to deal with Kinza's matted curls; and, arranged in a semicircle round them, squatted the whole village. They had turned out to a man to stare at this child, who apparently lived alone, like a rabbit, in the middle of a corn patch, and had accidentally strayed into their midst.

Hamid lay perfectly still, except that the sight of the cherries reminded him how hungry he was, and his hand stole to the loaf. He gnawed it thoughtfully; he was very ashamed of himself. They had lost a whole precious day in sleep and, worst of all, he had let Kinza escape into what might prove to be an enemy camp, unless he could retrieve her very quickly; for these people would certainly come to hear of the missing child from Thursday village. He dared not show himself; they might imprison him for skulking in their corn, and anyhow his only hope of rescue lay in remaining concealed.

So once again the sun went down, and moonlight flooded the village; then, when the world lay perfectly still, there was a tiny rustle in the corn. On silent feet Hamid crossed the open space, and stood poised in the doorway. The woman's husband lay on a mattress, snoring loudly, and his wife slept at his feet. There was no room for Kinza on the mattress, but she had been put to bed on a little mat near the door, and covered with a goat skin.

Hamid stooped down and gathered her up in his arms. She gave a little sigh, and half woke. He breathed her name urgently, and knowing all was well, she nestled up to him, clinging to him with all her strength. Neither buttermilk nor cherries had had any power to divide her loyalty. Although she had had a pleasant day, she knew something had been vaguely wrong. Now she was safely back in the tired arms of her brother; somehow from the moment he picked her up she slept more soundly than before. She had returned to her right place.

Five minutes later a gasping, frightened little boy with a thumping heart was hurrying up the hillside as fast as he could go, clutching Kinza against him. Not a villager had turned in his sleep, not a dog had lifted its head or barked. Noiseless as a ghost he had effected his rescue and Kinza had behaved perfectly.

Then, pausing for an instant to look about him, he saw a winding strip of stony road on his left, and made towards it. He looked up to the mountain towering above him, back to the valley and the river that led home. Hitching Kinza firmly on to his back, he set his face steadfastly toward the summit.

7

He reached the top just before dawn, limping, shivering, and unutterably weary. The nights on that high mountain pass were cold even in summer, and Hamid wore nothing but one coarse cotton gown. Kinza, too, snuggled closer to him, and began coughing and snuffling. He was too tired to go any farther for a while, so he squatted down on the lee side of the Spanish fort where sentries kept watch on the valley, and waited for morning.

The crest of the fort was just above him, and the road ran along a high ridge before it started on its downward course. On either side he could look down into deep valleys enclosed by mountains, and beyond the mountains were more mountains—range upon range of rocky peaks flushed by sunrise. Hamid felt as though he were standing alone on top of the world; in a place where no other human foot had ever trod.

There was one spot on the landscape that filled him with concern, and which he determined to avoid at all costs. At the far end of the ridge stood the Tuesday Market, a Spanish settlement with white government buildings, and plenty of idle soldiers on the look-out for mischief. If by any chance his father had reported him to the police the night before, they would certainly have 'phoned Tuesday Market to watch the paths. It was clear that he must leave the path, and make his way straight down the mountain side through the scrub bushes and olive groves until he reached the river in the valley some two thousand feet below. There he could sleep among the oleanders until sunset, when it would be safe to take the road again.

Binding Kinza on to his back again, he stepped out into the open and almost collided with two men on horseback, who had ridden up on the other side of the fort. They were on their way to Tuesday Market, and had travelled by night to escape the heat.

Hamid stood stock still and stared at them stupidly, too tired to act quickly. They were both from his own village and he knew them by sight.

The men stared at him for a moment; they had ridden straight into the sun, and were a little dazzled. Then one leaped lightly from his horse, and made a grab at Hamid.

" It's Si Mohamed's boy," he cried, " the one who was missing from Thursday Market the day before yesterday."

Hamid ducked and bolted down the mountain side. His sudden movement startled the horse, which reared in the air. The man, loth to let go of the reins, gave an angry shout, and the horse plunged forward. By the time the animal was properly under control Hamid was far away, leaping through the scrub, with Kinza bumping mercilessly behind him. Unconscious of thorns and roots, forgetful of his cut, bleeding feet, he went careering on, not daring to look behind, always expecting to feel a heavy hand laid on his shoulder and Kinza wrenched away from him.

The merchant, still clinging to the bridle, stood watching him. He had done his best, but he was not going to go chasing somebody else's brat all over the scrub bushes in his bright new yellow shoes with their pointed toes. It was none of his business, and he wanted to be in good time for market. He shrugged his shoulders, mounted his horse and rode on; he would tell the police at Tuesday Market. It was their job, not his, to hunt for runaway boys.

But poor Hamid, hearing in imagination terrible leaping feet behind him, went lumbering on, and Kinza, with her body nearly shaken to bits, gave jerky wails and hiccups on his back. He dared not stop running, and there seemed no refuge. Once he caught his foot in a root and fell headlong. Bruised and dirty, he was up in a second, and as he rose he noticed a rock jutting out ahead of him. He made for it blindly, rounded it, and found himself close to a thatched hut; and beside the hut was a mud goat-shed.

Hamid was quite certain that at any minute his enemy would appear round the rock, and this was his very last hope of escape. He sprang into the close dark shelter of the goat-shed, and found a sick goat and her kid lying on some straw. There was a pile of provender stacked against the wall, and Hamid burrowed into it. Then, like a hunted rabbit, he lay panting and shivering for half an hour.

At the end of that time, his heart was beating more normally, so he wriggled himself round in the straw, and began to take stock of the situation. From the house in front of the barn he could hear the sound of churning and the shrill prattle of little children, but otherwise all was quiet. His enemy had apparently not pursued him.

He himself felt very ill; he was burning hot, and his head ached dreadfully. His limbs were heavy and stiff, and the straw pricked and chafed his bleeding feet. They had had nothing to drink that morning, and his mouth was parched with fear and running. Kinza too was miserable, and wanted a drink. She had set up a pitiful sort of mewing, like that of a starved kitten, and her brother's pleadings were powerless to silence her. If anyone came to the barn, they would certainly hear her.

He looked round desperately, and then for the first time he began to consider the sick goat, which had broken its front leg some days before, and could not walk to pasture. His spirits went up at once, for here was the solution to their problems. Hamid understood goats, and a mother with a kid would have plenty of milk.

He wormed his way out of the straw, and, stealing to the doorway, grabbed hold of a piece of broken clay pot that had been thrown away. Then, with one eye on the house, he made friends with the goat, fondling her ears and letting her lick his hands. When she had finally recognized him as the expert that he was, he crept round behind her, and made friends with the kid. Then lying down on the floor beside it he milked the goat into the piece of shard, and carried the milk—sweet, warm, and frothing— to Kinza. She stuck her head out of her straw nest, drank it all up, and mewed for more. Hamid repeated the process a good many times, for the shard did not hold much, and both he and Kinza were parched and starving. They soaked hard pieces of bread in it, and Kinza enjoyed herself immensely, while the kind old goat gave ungrudgingly as though to an extra pair of kids. Once, while they were drinking, a very little girl came in and presented the goat with a bundle of new-mown hay; Hamid held his breath and pulled Kinza down in the straw, and the little girl, her eyes unaccustomed to the gloom, noticed nothing.

The excitement of milking, the pain in his feet, the stuffy heat of the straw pile, and the fever in his own body had kept Hamid wakeful all the morning. He was terrified of going to sleep too, because of Kinza's wandering propensities. He looked round for a piece of rope with which he might tether her to him, but there was nothing suitable, and he dared not come out till nightfall. Then sleep suddenly crept over him, dulling his reason and scattering his fears. He clasped her tightly to him, and knew no more.

But his tight grasp relaxed in sleep, and Kinza, taking his deep quiet breathing as a sign that she might now do as she pleased, wriggled out of his arms. She could not understand her brother's sudden liking for these prickly, tickly, hot places that made her sneeze. It was a liking she did not share in the least; and emerging from her hole, spluttering and indignant, she crawled off the provender heap.

Her private exploration yesterday had led her straight to a mother; today she was equally fortunate. She took a few uncertain steps and bumped straight into the goat.

She knew it was a goat instantly by its homely smell and the feel of its rough coat; and if there was one species of creation above all others which Kinza loved and felt perfectly at home with, it was the goat. She groped confidently for its ears and fondled them, after which she cupped her tiny hands round its nose. Then having found what she wanted—friendly company and a place to lie in which did not prick—she crawled under its beard and curled up to sleep, while the little kid, no doubt feeling jealous, also butted its way under its mother's chin. So they lay together, encircled by the goat's front legs: the new-born kid and the lost baby, equally content with their quarters.

Hamid, turning feverishly in his sleep, soon tossed away the straw and lay with his arms and face exposed. The day drew on, and towards sunset the mother of the prattling children came in with a bucket to milk the lame goat. For a moment she thought the creature had had another kid—then she looked more closely, and found it was a little girl curled up in a ball.

"May God have mercy on me!" exclaimed the woman. "It's a baby!"

She looked round in bewilderment, and caught sight of Hamid's top half sticking out of the straw.

"May God have mercy on my parents!" she cried out; "there's a boy as well!"

She strode vigorously over to him and prodded him with her leathery foot. She was a brawny woman, with broad cheek-bones and strong, bowed shoulders. Her voice was loud and strident, and she wanted an explanation quickly.

Hamid woke with a start and struggled into a sitting position. He was fuddled with sleep, but realized at once that wherever he was he was cornered and caught like a rat in a trap. His head still ached violently, and he lost all control of himself. He stuffed his knuckles into his eyes and began to cry.

"Stop it!" said the woman, slapping him on the back. "You are not from our village. Who are you? And where have you come from?"

Hamid gulped back his sobs, and looked at her. He had not the smallest objection to telling lies, but in this case he thought it might be an advantage to tell the truth. He had noticed that women were usually ready to take each other's part against husbands, unless, of course, they happened to be the wives of one man, and this woman would almost certainly side with his mother. So he told his story just as it stood, and she listened, frowning and nodding in turn.

When he had finished she looked at him approvingly. It was a good story and seemed true enough. She had been married twice, and her first husband had been very cruel to her and her child. He had divorced her when she was only fifteen years old, so she was quite ready to take up the cudgels against husbands in general. She, too, had known what it was to see her baby ill-treated, and she felt sorry for this unknown woman who was willing to risk so much for her blind child.

Besides all this, the woman had a motherly heart, and this bright-eyed boy who coughed as he spoke was obviously ill. About the filthy little bundle cuddling her goat she knew nothing as yet, but at least she could give her a better spot to sleep in. So she milked her goat, and then, with the bucket in her right hand and Kinza under her left arm, she strode to her house, with Hamid limping behind her.

The house was a circular mud-hut, rather dark inside, with a stack of winter bedding for the goats heaped against the wall. A clay pot bubbled on a fire, and three little girls sat round it expectantly. As they entered, the husband came down the mountain side with the flock, and they all gathered round to eat. Hamid, who had eaten nothing but bread and milk for two days, thought he had never tasted anything so good—a lentil stew, flavoured with garlic, oil, and red pepper—hunks of hot, soft bread to dip in it—a bowl of buttermilk from which they all drank in turn—and finally a dish of bruised apricots— the unbruised ones the father would carry to the Wednesday Market at dawn next day.

Hamid, eating and drinking deeply, felt his strength come back to him; for one night at least he would be safe and sheltered, and the peace of that knowledge cured his headache. The brawny countrywoman sat licking her fingers, and he gazed up at her as though she were a kind of angel from Heaven.

After supper the three little girls curled themselves up on goatskins against the hay, and went straight to sleep, in company with a cat and three kittens which also slept on a goatskin up against the hay. The father went out to milk, and his wife followed because she wanted to talk to him. Hamid, sitting by the fire with Kinza leaning up against him, could hear their voices. He supposed they were talking about him, and he was quite right, for the woman came back soon after with everything fixed up.

"Don't be afraid," she said encouragingly; "my husband is quite willing to help you. He is going into Wednesday Market tomorrow to sell apricots. He picks up a market lorry at the bottom of the hill just before daybreak. He will take you with him, and say you are my sister's children, for my sister lives on the road to Friday Market, where you are trying to get to, and she has a boy about your age and a baby girl. The lorry will drop you about 25 kilometres from Friday Market, on the main road, and you can probably get a lift—if not, it's not too far to walk."

She looked down at his joyful face, flushed in the firelight, and suddenly felt sorry because he was so young and helpless. Like Another long ago, she fetched a basin of water and a towel, and stooping down she washed his bruised, cut feet. Then she tore up a rag into strips, and bound up his wounds with olive oil; finally she laid him on one sheep-skin with his little sister, and covered him warmly with another. He fell asleep instantly, grateful and unafraid, and she went and sat very still on her door-step, her hands folded, looking out into the dusk.

8

TWENTY-FOUR hours later Hamid stood gazing up at the walls of the city he had come so far to seek, and feeling more lost than he had ever felt in his life before.

The journey had been lonely in parts, but after all Hamid was a shepherd, used to mountain solitudes. Wide skies and unpeopled distances held no terrors for him, and he was quite used to his own company. But this mass of humanity and mules and goats jostling each other in the town-gate, and the crowd of ragged children all perfectly at home, appalled him. His was the loneliness of the stranger—in the city, but not of it.

He had had a very successful day. He had woken at cock-crow, cool and refreshed; the woman had fed them and blessed them, and sent them forth into the dawn with her husband. At the bottom of the hill a lorry, jammed tight with market-goers and their wares, had picked them up and rattled off down the valley. Hamid had never been in a lorry before and the noise and speed and jolting thrilled him. He squatted in a corner, holding Kinza, trying to look like his benefactor's sister-in-law's son, and watching the river and the shut-in mountain landscape. The main road thrilled him too, with its roaring vehicles, and the two hours' drive passed all too quickly. The road turned off to Wednesday Market, and he and Kinza were dropped about fifteen miles from their destination.

He had walked all day, patiently plodding along in the heat, often sitting down to rest. At one point the river flowed parallel to the road, and here an idea had occurred to him. He had sat Kinza to sunbathe behind a bush, and washed her little dress as best he could, spreading it out to dry in the sun; for it struck him, when he looked at her critically, that nobody was going to be really pleased to see Kinza any more, unless she could be made a little cleaner. The result was encouraging, and Hamid redressed her, patted her tangles, washed her face, and decided she looked fit for a palace.

He had then climbed a long, long hill, with cornfields sweeping away to the valley and bright flowers nodding on the banks. He picked a bunch of poppies and scabious and blue bergamot for Kinza to present to her new mother, and toiled on gazing up at the mountain on his right. He did not like it. His own mountains were clothed with grass and rounded, with gentle slopes, but these were stark and bare, with summits of jagged rock. Yet the meadows at their skirts were greener than any meadows he had seen before, and the harvests more golden. He wondered why, and then forgot to wonder, for he had rounded a bend in the road and just ahead of him was the old city wall and the town inside—tier upon tier of lichened tiled roofs clustering round white mosques, rising steeply to the precipice rock behind them. Down below were the white buildings of the Spanish settlement built round a square.

Hamid stood in the cool shadow of the gate, and watched for a while. He did not think he would have to ask the way if he could once find the market, for his mother had described the house exactly, and he felt afraid to speak to anyone. He thought he would wait until nightfall before venturing along those narrow, crowded, cobbled streets. It would be easier to slip along in the dark. But as dusk deepened he saw the shopkeepers on each side of the street turn on the lights, and all who passed by walked in the full glare of them. Apparently in this terrifying place there was no darkness and no hiding. The sooner he could safely get rid of Kinza the better.

He set off timidly along the cobbles, marvelling at the beautiful wares displayed in the shops—the bright silks and highly-coloured sweetmeats, the piles of fruit and stacks of bread. It seemed to him like fairyland, and he gazed, bright-eyed and fascinated, at all this beauty—a magic town where everything glittered and dazzled, where perhaps no one was ever ill or sad or hungry or cold. He forgot he had felt lonely and afraid, and gazed up eagerly into the faces of the shopkeepers and passers-by. But no one smiled at him or looked kindly at him, and no one welcomed him to the golden city.

He crept along until he came to a splashing fountain where a little girl was filling buckets. She at least looked a kind little girl and very shyly he asked the way to the inn above the market. She pointed down some cobbled steps, gave him directions, and disappeared through her own front door.

It was not far to the inn. The old archway leading into the courtyard stood back from the street, but weary mules and donkeys were passing in and travellers stood in groups looking out on the market. Hamid longed to go and rest in the straw, because he would have felt at home with the donkeys, but he had no coin to pay for such shelter; and besides, he felt his business had better be done that night.

He was to go up the street directly opposite the inn. It was a very short street, ending in a wall; and the house, so his mother had said, was the very last on the left, with only a rubbish heap beyond it. It could not be difficult to find, and he set off confidently.

Then the street curved and he stopped. He could see to the end now, and what he saw filled him with surprise.

There was a dim street-lamp outside the last house on the left, and under it he could see a group of little boys, dirty and ragged like himself, standing expectantly. As Hamid watched, the house was opened from within, and a beam of bright light shone out on to the cobbles. At the turning of the key the children surged forward, tumbling over each other, and disappeared through the golden doorway. Then he heard other footsteps behind him, and three more little boys in black tatters sped past him on swift, bare feet; they too entered in. Then, as Hamid still stood in the shadows staring at the broad beam of light in the street, he heard the sound of singing—shrill unmusical singing it would have sounded to most readers of this story, but Hamid thought he had never heard anything so beautiful.

Lured by the music he crept closer, skulking along the wall, and at last he reached the step and dared to peep in. Then he caught his breath with joy and excitement, for he was looking across a passage-way into another room, and hanging on the wall of that room exactly opposite the doorway was the picture of the Man who loved little children, carrying in His arms a curly baby just about Kinza's age. Boys and girls were flocking round Him, holding out their arms, and He smiled down on them and did not seem to want them to go away. Hamid remembered the hard faces of the shopkeepers; this Man was unlike any of them. He would certainly welcome Kinza just as He was welcoming the crowd of happy children in the picture.

But who were all those ragged little boys? and why did they go in? and what were they singing about? He could not see them, for they all gathered at one end of the room, but he could hear a woman's voice speaking; and as he listened, crouching on the step, straining to catch the words, the children within began to chant something all together, as though they were learning it by heart, just as they did in the mosque schools when they learned the Koran.

Yes, he could hear what they were saying now—wonderful glowing words, brighter than any ever written in the Koran:

"Jesus said, I am the Light of the world: he that followeth Me shall not walk in darkness, but shall have the light of life."

What could it mean? Three times through they repeated the verse and Hamid whispered the words with them, and tucked them away in his memory to think about afterwards. The immediate problem now was, what to do about Kinza?

If all these children belonged to the nurse, she would certainly not want another; no little girls had entered the house, so perhaps the English, like his own people, on the whole preferred boys. Kinza's chances seemed very small if he knocked at the door and presented her as a gift. He must think of a better way than that.

Then a plan presented itself to him which he thought would almost certainly be successful, because his mother had said that the Saint in the picture had never been known to turn a child away. He would simply leave Kinza in the passage like a surprise parcel to explain herself as best she might and, if this nurse was really like her Saint, she would not throw such a tiny helpless creature homeless into the street on a dark night.

He skipped across the orange beam and established himself on the rubbish heap; he shook Kinza until she was thoroughly wide awake and then spoke to her very solemnly.

"Kinza, little sister," he said, "I am going to sit you down by yourself, and you must keep very still, and not cry. If you cry a lady will beat you hard. If you don't cry she will soon come and give you a nice sweet."

Now this was language that Kinza understood perfectly. She knew all about being hit if she did not keep still, and she seldom got what she wanted by crying. Also she was very hungry. So she submitted herself to being smoothed and patted and uncrumpled as much as possible, and then Hamid placed the withered bunch of flowers in her hand and crept off the rubbish heap. He pushed the door open another inch, lifted Kinza over the step, and sat her down in the dark passage.

All was perfectly quiet inside except for the voice within. Hamid suddenly felt his throat tighten and his eyes filled. Kinza would never be his own again, and he realized how much he loved her. As a sign of his love he drew out his last dry crust from the cloth, and thrust it into her hand; then he left her sitting cross-legged against the wall, very tousled and very crumpled, clasping a bunch of dead poppies and an old crust, for the surprise and delight of the unsuspecting missionary.

But through the blur of his tears he had caught sight once again of the face of the Man in the picture, and He seemed to be looking straight at Kinza. Hamid felt he had left his little sister sitting in the light of that smile, and it comforted him. Of course, the beams came through the open doorway of the lighted room, and it was only in his imagination that they streamed from the person of that Saint. Then, crouching against the wall of a little alley leading off the street, he tried to remember the words he had heard three times over: 'Jesus said, I am the Light of the World . . . instead of darkness you can have the light of life.' It was something like that, and whatever could it mean?

What was the light of the world? He thought of the lamp burning in his hut at home and the flickering shadows on the wall. He remembered the moonlit journey, and the circling stars, and the sunrise on top of the mountain. Moonlight, starlight, sunlight, candlelight, and the orange glare of the city street—they had all faded now. He was sitting alone in a very dark alley, and the moon had not yet risen behind the wall of rock. But Jesus said that instead of darkness you can have the light of life. "I am the Light of the World." He thought of Kinza and her perpetual darkness—could this light which he had never seen ever reach her? what did it all mean? If only it wasn't so dark . . . if only he wasn't so hungry . . . if only he could have kept Kinza . . . if only he could run home to his mother.

He stopped short in his thoughts, and leaned forward eagerly. A crowd of boys came hurrying down the street, and, at the corner, silhouetted against the window of a house, they turned to wave. They were talking eagerly, all at once, so Hamid could not hear what they said, but he caught odd phrases: "Who is she?"—"Such a little girl!" —"Where is her mother?" Then they passed out of sight, and the street was left in silence.

Then, prompted by his great longing to see what had happened, he tiptoed out of his alley, and prowled back to the rubbish heap. The door through which he had posted her was fast shut, and all was silence within. What had happened? There was a light in an upper window, and Hamid crossed the street and stood with his back pressed against the wall of the house opposite, gazing upwards; and as he stood looking there passed across the lighted window the figure of a woman nestling a little child in her arms, and the child showed no sign of fear. It neither struggled nor cried. It lay at peace with one little hand uplifted to feel the face bowed over it.

He had accomplished his errand and fulfilled his vow. All was well with Kinza. Not knowing where else to go, he slunk back to the rubbish heap, and covering himself as best he could with his rags, he curled up against the wall to sleep, with his head pillowed on his arm.

9

HAMID woke early next morning, stiff and cold, and blamed himself for his rashness in sleeping so near the house. Yet somehow it comforted him to know that Kinza was so close to him, only separated perhaps by one thickness of brick and plaster. He wondered whether she had woken yet, and what she was doing. He wandered along the street and out into the deserted market, wondering what to do, where to go, and above all where his breakfast was coming from. He had no doubt that Kinza was feeding on the fat of the land and rather regretted having given her that last crust.

It looked a golden city no longer. The shops were shuttered, and a few homeless beggars lay up against the temple steps, still fast asleep. Now that he had done all he had come to do, Hamid felt horribly flat and tired, and he stood in the middle of the market longing for home.

Then into the midst of his longing broke a familiar sound—the harsh rattle of a stork's cry and the rush of great wings sweeping over him, just as they used to do when he led his herd to pasture on his own dear mountains. He looked up quickly and saw her high up with the morning shining on her wings, flying to her nest in the grey turret of an old fort. The sight of her eased his loneliness a little, for the storks were part of home—only in his village they nested in the thatches and here their home was in a castle. He stared at the massive old walls and found that he was standing opposite an old gate in an archway leading into a garden.

The gate was wide open and there seemed no one to stop him. Hamid trotted across the cobbles, climbed the steps, and tiptoed through; he found himself standing in the most beautiful place he had ever seen in his life. It was a square garden enclosed in four grey walls over which the wistaria hung in great curtains. In the middle of it was a fountain, surrounded by green lawns and flower-beds, which were a scented mass of colour. Snapdragons, pansies, and stocks all grew in a riot, and behind them were rose bushes and orange trees in blossom. Never before had Hamid even dreamed of such beauty, and he stood fascinated with clasped hands, trying to take it all in. But in the midst of his ecstasy a keeper entered through the archway, and ordered him out. The town was beginning to wake up now, and men were unshuttering their stalls. Herdsmen were selling their milk, and as Hamid stood watching there was wafted to his nose a delicious smell of fried batter and hot oil. He was so hungry that something inside him seemed to turn right over, and he looked round eagerly to discover where it came from.

He had been standing with his back to a little stall where a man was frying dough-rings in a deep stone trough of oil. He seemed a busy man, for, as well as having to fish out the crinkly dough-rings and string them on to blades of grass for his customers, he was having to blow up the fire underneath—which appeared to put him in a bad temper, for he was muttering and growling a good deal.

Hamid drew as near as he dared to that delicious smell and stood first on one foot and then on the other. Then he suddenly had an idea: he walked boldly forward, feeling almost desperate with hunger, and asked the man if he needed an assistant.

The man looked him up and down. The boy who usually helped him had not turned up that morning and it was making life very difficult for Sillam, the doughnut-maker. He was prepared to accept help from the first boy who turned up, and Sillam had never seen this one before. He could not say that he actually knew him to be a rogue and a thief. He opened the wooden barrier and motioned Hamid inside.

"Take the bellows," he said, "and blow up this fire, and if I find you helping yourself to anything that doesn't belong to you, the police station is opposite!"

Hamid squatted down and began to blow. He did not feel very well; it was so hot the air swam and quivered round him, and the leaping flames scorched his face. He did not know that many little boys before him had been unable to stand the heat, and that he was pleasing the master by his quiet endurance. The fire roared upwards, the oil hissed and crackled in the cauldron. Then from what seemed a long way away he heard the master's voice saying, "Enough," and he staggered to his feet, dizzy and flushed.

"Now stand here, and thread the dough-rings on to the reeds," said the master, and Hamid leaned gratefully forward, taking deep breaths of air. He worked deftly enough, burning his fingers a little, but not minding much because he was too hungry to think about anything but the gnawing pains inside him. But he did notice that the market place was filling up, and that quite a crowd of tattered, grimy little boys were lounging about, watching him with searching eyes. He realized that somehow, before long, he would have to give an account of himself.

He had worked for about two hours, when the master suddenly said, "Have you had any breakfast?"

"No," said Hamid, "and, last night, no supper."

The master handed him a couple of hot, golden dough-rings. With a great sigh of relief Hamid sank his teeth into the first. It was wonderful. But the dark eyes of the little boys sitting on the cobbles became suddenly hostile. They were hungry, too, and this stranger was holding a coveted position.

Dough-rings are a breakfast food, and the shop shut at mid-morning. The master told Hamid he had worked well and might return early next day. Then he gave him a small coin, and Hamid, feeling like a little king, strutted across the market to decide how he would spend his wealth. He noticed a pile of sticky green sweets, and longed to buy one for Kinza. But Kinza probably no longer needed green sweets, and, in the comfort of her new home, had perhaps forgotten all about him. His throat suddenly felt a little tight. He resolutely stopped thinking about her, and turned his attention to the baker's shop.

It was then that a voice at his side said, "Who are you?" and he turned to see a little boy about his own age with a shaved, spotted head and a garment that had once been white, made from a printed sugar-sack. A strange little figure—but his dark eyes were bright and intelligent, and he looked at Hamid in quite a friendly way.

Hamid faced the little boy shyly. "I'm from the country," he replied.

"Why have you come to town?"

"To find work."

"Where are your father and mother?"

"Dead."

"Where do you live?"

"In the street."

The little citizen, whose name was Ayashi, nodded approvingly. "I too," he said cheerfully, "have no mother, and my father has gone to the mountains. I too live in the streets. We all do. Now buy us a loaf with the money the master gave you, and give us each a piece. Then you shall be one of us, and we will show you where we go for a supper at night."

His confident tone and his cheery acceptance of his homelessness fascinated Hamid. He would have flung his coin at the boy's feet in order to secure such a friendship. "You shall be one of us" were wonderful words; Hamid bought his loaf quickly and spent the change on a handful of black, bitter olives. Then he followed his patron to the eucalyptus tree in the middle of the square, where the gang squatted in the shade. He handed over the food to be divided up, and they fell upon it eagerly.

Hamid, with his portion, sat a little apart through shyness; but although no one said "Thank you," the gift had done its work. From that day onward he was truly one of them.

It was a strange gang to which, in his heart, he swore fealty that day—a gang bound together by a common bond of dirt, ignorance, and poverty; their uniform—rags and tatters; children who had never been loved. Tough and hardy they were, through much exposure; crafty and quick, through living by their wits. Thieving, lying, and swearing were regular habits, yet they still made the most of their pleasures.

Hamid, watching silently, swelled with pride, because he was sitting amongst them. He had never met boys like these, and he thought them wonderful—so tough and devil-may-care, so manly and independent. He longed to become like them, and he wriggled nearer.

He gathered that they earned their livings by various means. Some worked at looms certain days a week; and others, like himself, helped in the dough-ring shops. All begged between whiles, and hung round the hotel on the off-chance of carrying a bag for a tourist or watching a car. Some slept with their families at night in hovels called home, while others crept into the mosques. Life was uncertain and exciting, and there seemed only one event in their day which could really be depended on. That was their supper at the house of the English nurse.

Now they were all discussing the extraordinary things that had happened there on the previous night. It was a little stranger girl, they said, and none of them had ever seen her before. No one knew where she came from; she held up her arms to the English nurse and called for her mother, but she would not say anything else. So the English nurse had picked her up and taken her in, and today she was going to seek for the baby's parents.

"And what if she doesn't find them?" asked one little urchin. "Will she put her out in the street?"

Ayashi looked up quickly:

"She will not," he replied with complete confidence.

"How do you know? Why not? It is not her child!" exclaimed the other children in chorus.

"Because," answered Ayashi simply, "she has a clean heart."

10

THE rest of the day passed pleasantly. Ayashi, pleased by Hamid's admiration, took him round the town and up on to the hillside by the top gate to show him the spring of water welling up from the heart of the mountain through the cleft of a great rock. When all other streams fail through drought, this water, hidden so deep, goes on springing up in an ice-cold torrent, so that there are splashing fountains in the streets of the town, and a well-watered countryside. Hamid understood now why the fields had looked so green and the harvests so golden on the evening when he first entered the city.

At midday they hung round the door of the hotel; after a time a waiter flung them some broken rolls and meat that guests had left on their plates, and the boys fell upon them like hungry dogs. Then they curled themselves against the trunk of the eucalyptus tree and slept in the shade.

Evening came, the sun set behind the turret of the fort, and the mother stork stood on one leg, clear-cut against a rosy sky. Hamid stuck close to Ayashi, and they sat on some steps together with a few friends watching the country people crowding into the square. Tomorrow was market day, and those who had come from a distance would out their sacks against the wall and sleep beside their wares. As darkness fell the shopkeepers kindled their lamps again, and other litttle boys sauntered up from their various employments and collected on the steps.

"Come," said Ayashi, who seemed to be a sort of leader among them, " she will soon open her door now."

He motioned Hamid to follow him, but Hamid hesitated. He felt torn in two; hunger and his great longing to see whether all was well with his little sister urged him on, but caution held him back. What if he should be forced to speak while Kinza was there? She would certainly recognize his voice and run to him, and that would arouse everyone's suspicion.

"Come on," called Ayashi impatiently, looking back.

Hamid shook his head. "I'm not coming," he replied and sat down again on the steps, with his head in his hands, staring gloomily into the market. He had been fairly happy all day long in Ayashi's company, but now he forgot Ayashi in his overwhelming longing for his mother and Kinza. But then he got up, because he had suddenly had an idea. He would not go in, but he would creep to the door of the house, as he had done on the night before, and peep through a crack. Perhaps he would catch a glimpse of Kinza, or see her again against the orange window upstairs. Like some guilty little thief he darted into the quiet back street and sneaked along the wall towards the open door and the beam of light.

He peered round very cautiously, but there was no sign or sound of her—only the murmuring voices, and then the shrill cracked noise of little boys singing. Kinza apparently was nowhere about, and he was standing in a very dangerous position. He shuffled on to the rubbish heap, and began to cry quietly because his friends and his little sister had all entered in through the open door that led to shelter and light and food—and he was left outside.

And then something happened. The door opened a little farther, and the nurse stepped out into the street to see if any more were coming along before she started the lesson. She appeared silently, and Hamid did not see her at first. But she heard a wretched, sniffing sound close at hand and looked round.

She saw a desolate little outcast huddled on the rubbish heap with its knuckles in its eyes, and she took a step nearer. He heard her footfall and started up frightened. But she stood between him and freedom and he could not escape, so he rubbed away his tears and crouched staring up at her. He had never seen anyone like her before.

"Why don't you come in?" she asked.

Lured by a sense of welcome, he got up and advanced slowly towards her. She waited quite still, afraid of startling him. Then, when he was close to her, she held out her hand. He took it and stepped trustfully over the threshold.

They entered the lighted room together, and Hamid stood in the doorway taking a good look round. It was a long whitewashed room, furnished Moorish fashion with a rush mat on the floor and mattresses against the wall. At one end were a table and some shelves with rows of bottles on them, and at the other end the boys sat cross-legged in a semicircle. On the wall opposite the door was the picture of the Saint smiling down on these waifs of the street, just as He had smiled down on Kinza.

"Come," said the nurse, "sit down with the others. I'm going to show you something."

Ayashi grinned at him delightedly, and Hamid wormed his way into the semicircle so as to sit beside him. He wished they would sing again, because he wanted to hear what they were singing about, but apparently the singing was over, and they were all waiting for the nurse to show them something. Hamid glanced at their expectant faces and felt less in awe of them than he had felt all day. They looked somehow younger, not like men of the world any more.

The nurse sat down on the mattress in front of them, and showed them a strange little book. It was quite unlike the Koran, which was the only book Hamid had ever seen inside, and it had no writing in it at all—which was just as well, because not one of the audience could read a letter. It had only four blank pages in it and each page was a different colour.

The first page was shining gold and very beautiful, and as the nurse held it up in front of them she spoke of a golden city bright with the light of the love of God, and Hamid thought of his first night in the town when the lamps had shone out in the dark. But in spite of the lamps there were hunger and sickness and loneliness and unkindness in their town, while in the City of God, so said the nurse, there were none of those things—only pure joy and brightness and goodness.

"I'd like to go there," thought Hamid; "it would be even better than our village—no fear, no quarrelling, no blindness."

But while he was thinking about the Golden City the nurse turned to a black page and told them it was like the darkness and the sadness of hearts that had done wrong. Hamid had never worried about doing wrong before—in fact, had never even thought what wrong was. Of course, he stole if he got the chance, and naturally he told lies if they would save him a beating—why shouldn't he? Well, one reason seemed to be that no darkness could ever enter the Golden City of Light, and the gate was shut to sin.

Hamid looked thoughtfully round the semicircle—how very black they all were! Their rags and their hands and faces and feet were black with dust and grease and mud. Their hearts, said the nurse, were also black with lies and bad words and blows and stealing. That was a pity, thought Hamid, and he had a vision of a host of dirty little boys being turned away from the gates, and creeping back into the shadows.

But that was not the end. The nurse turned to a red page, and told them a very strange story. Apparently God's Son, whose name was Jesus, loved boys, and actually wanted them in His bright city. So He had come down into the world to live with them, and then at the end He had died to bear a punishment for sins He had never done Himself. It was the children who had sinned, and Jesus who had been punished, and the red page meant that He had died a cruel death, and the red blood had flowed from His body—and it did not seem right at all, because *He* had not done anything wrong. It was the children who really deserved the punishment.

The best of this story was that, because Jesus had been punished, bad, thieving children could be forgiven. If they turned from sin and asked to be forgiven because Jesus had taken their punishment, their black hearts would be made just like the next page—and the next page was spotless white; they would be made white enough to walk right into the light of the Golden City, and even that radiance would discover no spot. They could be made perfectly pure and clean. Hamid forgot about himself and his friends—he thought of the orange-blossom petals transparent with the brightness of the sun, and the wings of the stork when the light touched them. Then he forgot all about everything, for the nurse had stopped talking and was bringing in two great bowls of steaming rice and handing round hunks of bread. The children broke into two groups and huddled over their supper, scooping up the food at an amazing pace, and then polishing the bowls with their dirty little fingers. No one spoke much until the last lick and crumb had vanished because they were racing each other to get the most, but when all had gone they sat back on their heels and questioned the nurse about the little girl whom they had found in the passage the night before.

" She is still with me," said the nurse, smiling a little, as though she had remembered something funny. " She is, at this moment, asleep in bed."

Hamid looked at her hard. She did not seem annoyed at Kinza's being still with her.

" I have taken her all round the town with me today," went on the nurse, " but nobody has ever seen her before, or knows who her parents are. She is a little blind girl, so I suppose no one wants her."

" And what will you do with her?" asked the boys, all together.

" Well, I shall have to keep her for the moment; there's nothing else to be done," said the nurse. This time she laughed outright, and Hamid nearly laughed too, with joy and relief. He had a wild, reckless longing to see his little sister asleep in bed, and he was no longer afraid. He waited until the little boys had bowed and shaken hands with their hostess and skipped off into the dark. Then she turned and found him lingering in the passage. His heart was beating violently, but he spoke steadily and boldly.

"I come from a village," he said, "and in my village there are two or three blind baby girls whose parents come into market. Let me see her, and perhaps I can tell you who her mother is."

The nurse looked down at him, surprised; she had certainly never seen this little boy before, and he might be speaking the truth. She had watched him since he entered her house, and noticed his thin, tired face, and his bruised feet—also the ravenous way he had fallen on his food. She guessed he had travelled a long way, and was glad to shelter him, so she led him to a room upstairs, to where Kinza lay on a mattress fast asleep.

She looked different because she had had a bath and had come out quite another colour. Also her hair had been washed and cut, and instead of her gollywog tangles she had soft dark curls clustering over her forehead. Her old dress had been changed for a little white nightgown, spotlessly clean. Surely, thought Hamid, she is clean enough even to stand in the light of the Heavenly City, clean as a white flower; he gazed at her, fascinated for a while, and then turned to take notice of her surroundings. The room was furnished simply, native style, but there were pretty covers on the mattresses, books on the shelves and pictures on the walls. It was a brightly lit room, too, and he felt as if Kinza had somehow passed beyond him, through golden gates into a new land of light. He yearned to stay with her, but he knew it could not be.

"I do not know her," he said gravely, rising to go. "She is not one of the children from our village."

He followed the nurse downstairs in silence, and she came to the door and let him out. He stepped into the street, and then, standing on the boundary of light and darkness, he looked up into her face and took hold of the hand that had been so kind to Kinza.

"You are good!" he said simply. "Your food is good; your teaching is good; your heart is good; may God have mercy upon your ancestors!"

Then he bounded away down the street, and the darkness swallowed him up.

11

HAMID kept his post in the doughnut shop and became a satisfactory little assistant. He worked hard, and his master was usually quite kind to him, giving him his breakfast and his coin regularly. The coin he spent on dinner, and the nurse provided him with his supper. He slept with Ayashi just inside the mosque, and as long as the sun shone and the weather kept warm he was happy. Life was gay and varied and there was plenty to do. During the harvest they went down to the fields and helped carry the bundles to the threshing-floor till darkness fell, and then they went to sleep on a heap of chaff. Later on they hired themselves out to pick olives, stuffing as many as they could into their mouths without being seen. On hot days they went bathing in the rocky stream that flowed from the spring in the mountain, and washed all their dirt away.

Five days a week they went to the house of the English nurse, and squatted on the mat to hear a story about Jesus, and to have supper. Hamid knew quite a number of stories now. He knew that Jesus was not a Saint at all, but the Son of God, and had come down into the world. He knew that the lame and the blind had flocked to Jesus, and He had healed them. Hamid wished that he also had lived then, for he would have carried Kinza to the Saviour, and her eyes would have been opened. He knew that Jesus had died with His arms stretched out in welcome on a cross, and like their own saints He had been placed in a rocky tomb—but with this difference: their own saints remained in their tombs to be visited every year, but Jesus had not been bound by death. He had come to life again and left His tomb, and had been seen in a beautiful garden, like the castle garden at sunrise, on the first day of the week.

He knew too that Jesus had gone back to the Golden City of Light and was still alive at the right hand of God, and that the living Spirit of Jesus was willing to enter into the hearts of boys, to make them good. Once the nurse spoke about Him knocking at the door of their hearts, and Hamid laid his small dirty hand across his chest under his rags.

"I can hear Him," he said very seriously: "He is knocking at mine . . . tap! tap! tap!"

But the nurse explained that that was only his own heart beating, and that the knocking of the Lord could not be felt with hands, nor heard by ear. It was the longing that came over us to open that made us know He was knocking; but Hamid by this time was wondering what they were going to have for supper, and he had lost interest in the subject for the time being.

Summer drew into autumn, and the nights became colder and longer. There were no more tourists at the hotel now, so there were no cars to watch and no luggage to hold; these had given quite a lot of money to Hamid and his friends during the summer, but now they must sharpen their wits and tighten their belts. Ayashi taught Hamid the queer, unchildlike beggars' cries, and they would tramp round together in the rain, wailing at the studded wooden doors of rich people's houses. Sometimes they collected a good many scraps of food, sometimes nothing. It was all very uncertain, like the November weather and the temper of the dough-ring man. The only comfort in life that could really be depended on was supper at the house of the English nurse.

She lit a charcoal brazier for them these nights, and let them in early. They would troop across her hall, their rags dripping, leaving a trail of black water and footprints on the tiles. Then they would huddle round the glowing coals to warm their blue fingers, and gradually their teeth would stop chattering. Then they would sit back, steaming a little, but content—and happy to listen to anything their friend might wish to say.

Clothes were a great problem just now. The wind and rain pierced and rotted their rags, and Hamid sometimes wondered just how much longer his flimsy summer garment would hold together, as he saw no prospect of replacing it when it finally fell to pieces. Some of his friends had begged or stolen sacks which they wrapped round them, but Hamid had not been one of the fortunate ones.

Kinza, on the other hand, had no clothes problem. She always went shopping with the English nurse, and Hamid often saw her waddling across the market on legs that had grown amazingly fat and sturdy during the past two months. Over her clean Moorish gown she wore a red woolly jersey and a little brown cloak. She had rubber shoes on her feet and a woolly hood over her dark curls. She looked the picture of health and happiness, and Hamid, edging up as close as possible, felt very proud of her.

The rain was sheeting down mercilessly one night when the children splashed their way up the running cobbles and hammered at the door of their refuge. They shook themselves on the step like wet little dogs, and surged forward toward the fire, puffing and blowing and sniffing. The English nurse felt a pang as she watched them, for she thought she had never seen them looking more wretched, more mud-bespattered, more at enmity with life. Yet the faces lifted to hers were still merry and impudent, and the dark eyes were still bright; she marvelled at their unconquered courage.

But there was one well-known little figure missing, and this was the second night he had not turned up—an undersized shrimp of a boy who had been most regular for months past. "Where is Abd-el-Khader?" asked the nurse. "Why hasn't he come these two nights?"

"He can't come," replied one child in a careless voice. "His rags fell right to pieces, and he hasn't a father. He has nothing to wear at all, and he must stay at home till his mother can save enough to buy a sugar-sack."

No one showed any concern or surprise, and the evening passed as usual. But when supper was finished she turned to Hamid, who always lingered to the last. "Do you know where Abd-el-Khader lives?" she asked.

Hamid nodded. "Up at the top of the town by the prickly pear hedges," he replied; "but the path is like a muddy river. You could not go there tonight."

"I think I could," said the nurse, "and if you would like to earn a few gourdas, you can take me there."

Hamid nodded enthusiastically. A few gourdas were worth any amount of battling with rain and mud, and, besides, he liked Abd-el-Khader. He waited at the bottom of the stairs while the nurse went upstairs to unpack a bundle of old clothes, and while he waited his bright inquisitive eyes roamed round the premises. He had never been left alone before, and he found it very interesting. He poked his nose into the room on the left and found himself in a little kitchen with shelves on the walls and an oil stove. On one shelf stood a china basin of eggs, just low enough for him to help himself.

Hamid hesitated; he could not count, but perhaps the nurse could, and would notice if he took two. On the other hand, raw eggs sucked through a little hole in the top are delicious, and Hamid had not tasted one for a long time; he thought on the whole it was worth the risk. If he waited outside the door, the nurse would never see in that rain-driven darkness; even if she noticed later she could not exactly prove it was he.

So he took one in each hand, nipped out into the street, and stood waiting in the dark. He did not wait long. The nurse soon appeared with a bundle and a key, and, what Hamid had not bargained for, a powerful torch. Little boys who prowl the streets at night develop cat's eyes, and do not reckon with such things.

"Come along," said the nurse, turning on her torch. "Come and get under my coat, and we can both walk in the light."

But to the nurse's surprise Hamid did not wish to walk in the light. He seemed to be taking great care to keep out of the beam, slinking along the gutters, shuffling against the wall. It was very dark and very muddy, and once or twice he slipped a little, clutching his precious eggs tightly in both hands.

"Why won't you walk with me in the middle of the road?" asked the nurse, puzzled. "You will fall if you run along in the gutter like that."

"I'm all right," muttered Hamid, rather miserably. He was not enjoying himself at all. He was so afraid of that broad beam of light, and the eggs somehow did not seem worth it. He wished he could get rid of them, and yet at the same time he wanted to hold on to them.

The light of the lamp made the surrounding darkness pitch black, and when they started climbing the steep back-alleys Hamid could not see where he was going at all. Suddenly he caught his foot on an unexpected step and fell violently forward on his face; he gave a sharp cry of shock and pain, and the nurse, who was a little ahead, turned round quickly and switched the light full on to him.

She saw him struggle to his feet, his garment covered with black mud and yellow egg-yolk. She saw his hands clasping the smashed shells, and his grazed knees streaming with blood, and she understood at once what had happened. He would have scuttled away from her, but she took hold of him quickly, and he burst into frightened tears. He had no idea what she would do. She might fetch the police and put him in prison; or she might beat him in the street. Whatever she did or did not do, she certainly would never have him in her house again. He had forfeited his right to the only shelter left to him on earth. Never again would he enter that place of warmth and light; he was shut out, and it was all his own fault.

Then through his sobs he heard the voice of the nurse speaking quietly to him.

" Come along," she said; " you've cut your knees badly. We'll go home and bind them up, and then you can show me the way again afterwards." She kept tight hold of him, and they walked home in silence, except for Hamid's sniffs. There was a lull in the rain, they re-entered the quiet, warm house, and she locked the door on the inside.

Still silent and ashamed, he washed his hands under the tap, and then the nurse told him to sit down. She fetched a basin of warm water and bathed his black knees till the cuts and grazes were quite clean. Then she bound them up with ointment and white bandages, and when she had finished she took a good look at him. He sat slumped in a sorry little heap covered with mud and raw egg. The only clean parts about him were the little tracks on his cheeks where his tears had made furrows through the grime.

Still without speaking she went upstairs to the bundle of old clothes and came back with a clean shirt, and a much-darned grey woolly jersey. Then she fetched more warm water and soap, and scrubbed him clean all over. Next she dressed him in his new clothes, and sat down beside him.

He looked up at her, marvelling, for it was his very first experience of anyone returning good for evil, and he could not understand it. Instead of prison and a beating he had been given medicine and clean, beautiful clothes.

" Hamid," said the nurse beside him, " you fell over and hurt yourself because you would not walk in the light with me. You were afraid to walk in the light because you had stolen my eggs."

There was no answer.

"You don't deserve ever to come here again," went on the nurse, "but they were my eggs and I paid for them, so I'm going to forgive you—only you must promise never to steal anything out of my house again."

Hamid nodded.

"And remember," said the nurse, speaking very slowly and earnestly, "you could not walk with me in the light, because of your sin. The Lord Jesus says He is the Light of the World. He asks you to walk beside Him all the way and every day until you reach His beautiful bright home. But first you must tell Him about your sin, and ask Him to wash away all its stains and make you clean, just as I washed away the mud and the egg. Then you must leave it behind for ever, and keep beside Him in the light."

Hamid looked down at his clean clothes and his spotless bandage, and understood. His eggs that had seemed so precious were gone, but he did not want them any more. He had been forgiven and washed and made clean. He had been brought back into the warmth and shelter of the nurse's home. They were going out again in the dark to find Abd-el-Khader's house, but it would be quite different now. He would get under the nurse's big, warm coat and walk close beside her, sheltered from the rain; he would not stumble, and he would not be afraid of the light any longer, because he no longer had anything to hide. They would walk guided by its bright, steady beam. It would be a treat.

Half an hour later, having accomplished their errand, they returned to the house. The wind roared against the rocks behind the town, and the rain beat up the streets in cold gusts. Hamid, warm and quite comforted, popped out from under the nurse's coat, and said goodbye on the step.

"But where are you going to sleep?" asked the nurse doubtfully.

"In the mosque," answered the little boy.

"But have you any blankets there?"

" No."

" Is it not very cold?"

" Tonight I shall be warm in my jersey."

" Well, you can come in tonight and sleep on the dispensary floor. The fire is still burning."

So she left him, lying comfortably on the mat, covered with a blanket, staring into the glow of the dying charcoal and thinking over the events of the evening. He had learned something that night that he would never forget all his life, and sitting up suddenly he held out his cupped hands after the Moslem fashion of prayer, and whispered the simple hymn that all Moroccan children who are taught by missionaries know by heart. They repeat the first line of each verse three times over, and the words in English go like this:

> *Give me a clean heart,*
>   *O my Lord and my God.*

> *Take away my sins from me,*
>   *In the blood of my Saviour.*

> *Lead me to Heaven,*
>   *To Your house, O God.*

12

HAMID and Ayashi crept shivering from the mosque one morning to find the olive groves and mountains above the town white with snow. The winter season had come to stay.

One week was particularly cold and bleak, and on a night of drizzling rain the children arrived at the door as usual and knocked impatiently, for the wind seemed to be cutting them in two, and their sodden, fluttering rags clung to their bodies. The door was opened at once, and they tumbled over the threshold, eager to reach the warmth of the fireside. But once inside the passage they stood arrested and staring, the cold and the rain forgotten.

For instead of the bright glare of electric light, they found themselves facing the soft blaze of candles set circle-wise on a little table in the middle of the room, with silver boughs of olive wreathed round them. On the floor, arranged like a picnic on a coloured cloth, a feast was spread. There were nuts, almonds, raisins, sweets, oranges, bananas, sugar biscuits and honey cakes, and on a tray in the corner a shining teapot and a collection of little glasses. A kettle sang merrily on the glowing charcoal, and the room seemed warm and welcome. Even Kinza had stayed up to the feast. She sat on a cushion, holding a big red-and-white rubber ball, her face lifted expectantly.

"It's the Feast of the Christians today," explained the nurse to the wide-eyed little boys, "so I thought we would keep it together. It is the Feast of the birth of Jesus Christ. He was the greatest gift God ever gave, so at His Feast we all give presents to each other. That is why Kinza has a rubber ball, and that is why I've bought you sweets and oranges and bananas."

The children sat down to their feast, a little awed at first by the strangeness of the silver light and their own pleasure; but gradually their tongues loosened, their toes and fingers thawed, and their cheeks flushed. They talked and ate merrily, tucking away their fruit and sweets in their rags to eat later, and sipping glass after glass of sweet, hot mint tea.

Hamid could not take his eyes off Kinza. She was dressed in her very best blue smocked frock and her curls were brushed out like an aureole. How round and sturdy she had grown! He suddenly remembered the white-faced, ragged little sister of past winters, the mud in the village, and the poverty and wretchedness. All that seemed shut out now; they seemed to be sitting cut off from the bleak world outside, in a warm kind circle of candlelight. The children were talking about feasts in general, and he began to talk too. He began telling them about the sheep feast in his own village, and the nurse, watching his eager face, felt glad. He too had changed lately. He had never told her what had happened to him the night he took the eggs, but his manner was so different these days. He was no longer a shy, hesitating little stranger; he took his place confidently and expectantly every night, and his whole being seemed to respond to the story of the Saviour's love. So she sat watching him, longing to know what had taken place in that child-heart; until her attention was suddenly caught by a little drama going on at her side.

Kinza had risen to her feet, and there was a look on her face the nurse had never seen before. It was a look of dawning, half-perceived memory, as though she had heard some dearly-loved but forgotten sound. Then, groping a little uncertainly, feeling her way with touch and hearing almost as sensitive as sight, she moved towards the speaker, and stood beside him, irresolute, tense.

At any other time Hamid would have been frightened at his secret being discovered, and would probably have pushed Kinza away. But there was an atmosphere in the room that night that cast out fear and suspicion, and Hamid, forgetful of everyone else, put his arm round his little sister, and drew her to him, while she, not knowing who he was, but somehow stirred and drawn by the voice she had once loved, nestled up to him, and laid her shining head comfortably against his wet rags. And the nurse, watching in amazement, suddenly noticed how astonishingly alike they were. A number of little incidents that had seemed unimportant up to now, flashed into her mind: the almost simultaneous appearance of the two children from nowhere; Hamid's strange request to see Kinza asleep, and the secretive way he had watched her in the street. She suddenly felt quite sure that they were brother and sister; but, even if she were right, it was of no practical importance. Hamid was unlikely to betray his secret, and she on her side had no intention of parting with Kinza. She could only guess what sad misfortune had cast these two little wanderers adrift into the world, and marvel at the loving-kindness that had led them to the haven of her own home.

The other children stared too. "She knows his voice," they said wonderingly, and they too glanced at each other with surprise. But they would not speak their thoughts in front of the nurse, and soon forgot about it in further glasses of mint tea. Then, the feast being ended, the nurse made them turn round and look at a white sheet hung on the wall. She blew out the guttering candles, and pictures appeared in the dark. The boys thought it was magic, and watched wide-eyed and open-mouthed.

It started with a picture of a girl knocking at the door of an inn, but she had to go away because there was no room. Hamid felt sorry for her, because he, too, on his first night in town, had stood and gazed into the inn, longing for shelter. He had had no money, so he had slept on the rubbish heap, but the woman had gone into a stable, and the next picture showed them installed among the oxen. But a wonderful thing had happened. She had brought forth her first-born Son, and swaddled Him, just as his own

mother had swaddled Kinza, and laid Him in a manger.
Kinza had had a wooden cradle, he remembered, but this
Baby was the child of very poor people, no doubt—home-
less outcasts like himself.

But what was the nurse saying? The Baby in the manger
was the Lord Jesus Christ, in honour of whose birth all
Christians kept the feast of giving. He was God's great gift,
and He had come willingly. The stable in the picture looked
rather dark, lit only by one small lantern, but the home of
the Son of God in Heaven was bright with the light of
glory and love. Why had He left it?

The nurse was just telling them: "Though He was rich,
yet for your sakes He became poor." He left the light and
came into the dark, a homeless, outcast Child, in order to
lead homeless, outcast children to the shelter and love of
His Father, God.

And now there was a third picture: there were shepherds
on the hillside keeping watch over their flocks by night;
and Hamid thought of his own goats, and the days he had
spent with them on the mountain—but here was another
picture: the Angel of the Lord appeared, and the glory of
the Lord shone round about them. They were afraid; but
apparently the sheep were not. They seemed to be grazing
quietly in the bright shelter of the Angel's wing. "Unto
you is born a Saviour," said the Angel to the assembled
company, and even the open heavens and the singing hosts
failed to alarm the flock. Hamid suddenly remembered the
anguished cries of the sheep dragged to their slaughter on
the first day of the sheep feast. But here was no crying
and no slaughter. There was peace in Heaven and goodwill
on earth.

Then the last picture was flashed on the screen. The
shepherds had left their flock to the care of the Angel, and
here they were, barefoot, in their rough fleece coats, kneeling and worshipping at the manger. Hamid again thought
of the sheep feast; the rich and the great of their land
gorging themselves with fine food, and flinging what was

over to the beggars and the dogs. But this was their very own feast. It was Kinza's feast, because Jesus had become a little Child, wrapped in swaddling clothes and it was his feast because the King of Heaven had become homeless and had been laid, outcast, among the cattle.

It was over. The nurse switched on the lights, and the pictures faded. There was nothing visible left of the feast but gutted candles, sweet-papers, orange-peel and banana-skins. But the thought of a love that gave, and of a love that became poor, lingered with Hamid as he stepped out thoughtfully into the wet street. Kinza stood in the door-way, waving to the sound of their retreating footsteps, and as he passed he put out a shy hand and touched her hair.

The other boys had gone on ahead, but Hamid loitered along slowly, the pictures still bright in his head, un-conscious of the drizzling rain. As he passed under a blurred street-lamp a sharp little mewing caught his ears, and he looked down and saw a skeleton-like kitten, very small and wet, trying to shelter behind a drain-pipe.

In his eleven years of life he had seen many starving kittens dying in the street, and had never given them two seconds' thought. But tonight it was somehow different. He could not possibly have explained, but he had just been drawn close to a Child who was lowly and gentle and com-passionate, and all unknown to him the first seeds of gentleness had been sown in his heart. He found to his surprise that he cared about the starving little creature, and he picked it up and held it against him. It was so thin that its skin seemed to be stretched tightly over its bones, and he could feel its rapidly thumping heart.

What should he do with it? He had no doubts at all. There was one open door where it would certainly be welcome, and Kinza would probably love it. It would be his Christmas gift to her.

He pattered back over the wet cobbles and knocked at the nurse's door. When she opened it, he held out the shivering, wretched creature with perfect confidence.

"It is for Kinza," he explained, "a gift of the feast. It is very hungry and cold, so I brought it to you."

The nurse hesitated. The last thing she really wanted just then was a half-dead ginger kitten, covered with sores and vermin, but she could not refuse, because of what lay behind the gift. With a thrill of joy she realized that her evening's work had not been in vain. One little boy at least had understood, and entered into the spirit of Christmas. He had wanted to give, and he had been gentle and kind to an outcast kitten. It was the first time in all her experience that she had seen a Moorish child care about the sufferings of an animal.

So she accepted it gratefully and joyfully, and then holding it at arm's length she carried it to a box near the fire and sprinkled it all over with a disinfectant powder. Then she gave it a saucer of milk, and it twitched its tail at an impertinent angle, and lapped it up—a tough, gallant little kitten, unconquered by adversity! It deserved to be saved.

As she sat watching it she had a sudden vision, which passed swiftly and left her laughing. She thought she saw all the Christmas love-gifts of all the ages heaped together before the manger—the gold, the frankincense, the myrrh; the stars, the homage of heaven, the treasure and worship of earth. And perched on top of the glittering pile, precious in the eyes of the One to whom it was given, was a thin, flea-ridden, ginger kitten, with its tail at an impertinent angle—the first-fruits of a little boy's compassion.

PART TWO

13

MANY, many miles away, under different Christmas stars, another party was in progress. It had this much in common with the party in the Nurse's house—the children at each were radiantly, gloriously happy, and thought life left nothing to be desired.

Otherwise it was a quite different kind of party. Instead of oranges and nuts and sweets there were jellies and trifles and chocolate biscuits, and a big Christmas cake; and instead of black, wet rags there were bright-coloured dresses and jerseys, and the girls had gay ribbons in their hair. It should have been a perfect party, and yet when the tea and games were over, and the joyful children gathered under the Christmas tree to sing carols, the grown-up visitors all felt sad, and one small visitor of nine years old felt saddest of all.

For this was a Blind School, and the little singers with their bright faces lit up by the candles could not see the tree or the soft lanterns or the toys they had been given. They had eaten their meal with enormous relish, and danced merrily up and down to the sound of music, and now they were singing with all their hearts and souls; and Jenny, sitting with her mother and father in the audience, found she had a lump in her throat. If she always had to live in the dark she was quite certain she would never be happy again. She shut her eyes for a moment, and tried to imagine what it would be like to be blind, but it was really too dreadful even to think about, so she opened them again quickly, and watched the children.

They were singing a carol now—one that Jenny herself had learnt at school:

Star of wonder, star of light,
Star with royal beauty bright,
Westward leading, still proceeding,
Guide us to thy perfect Light.

And Jenny, who was a practical child, wondered why
they had been taught such words. What was the good of
singing about perfect light when they were doomed to
spend all their days in darkness? Yet, as she watched them,
she had to own to herself that not one little singer looked
unhappy; the lifted shining faces seemed almost as though
they had caught sight of that Christmas star, and the
perfect Light beyond it—very far away, but clear in the
distance.

Jenny knew the story of that carol, and when they had
decorated the form-room at her school for their Christmas
party they had made a beautiful model frieze, sticking
the figures on dark blue paper to represent a night sky.
They had all helped to colour and cut out the figures, and
their form-mistress had stuck them on one by one: three
lurching camels with bright trappings, and three wise
men with long white beards and beautiful flasks and
caskets of treasures—the gold, the frankincense and the
myrrh; a shining star up above, beaming down on a
humble little house where a lowly woman sat playing
with her baby Boy, who was, in some strange way that
Jenny could not understand, the Perfect Light toward
which they were travelling.

Her mother touched her, because the carols were over
and everyone was clapping—except for Jenny, whose
thoughts were far away. She came back to earth with a
start, and began clapping very loudly, so that the blind
children should see how pleased she was, until her mother
signed to her to stop because someone wanted to make a
speech. And then it was all over, and the children surged
round to say goodbye, touching and feeling and chattering, and the 'littlest ones' were borne away happy and
sleepy to bed. But the bigger ones thronged the doorway

to wave and shout to the sound of the cars driving away; and that was the last Jenny saw of them—a mass of rosy, laughing faces and waving hands.

She was very quiet on the way home, and her mother, thinking she was tired, hurried her up to her room, lit her gas fire, and bustled her into bed. For Jenny had been ill, and this was her first real outing for three months. Her mother had wondered whether she ought to go, but Jenny had insisted, and as usual had got her way. Her father had recently joined the Council of the Blind School and they had all been invited to the Christmas party.

She nestled down under her pink satin eiderdown and surveyed her beautiful array of Christmas presents—the books, the games, the cosy new dressing-gown, the little gold wrist-watch and the travelling case. It had been a very satisfactory Christmas, and the best present of all— a pony of her very own—was down in the stable. For the first time in her rather self-centred little life it suddenly occurred to Jenny, as she lay waiting for her mother to bring her goodnight drink, that she was really a very fortunate child. She thought of the blind children with the toys they could not see, and the children out in Morocco who had no toys at all, and often no food. Her Aunt Rosemary looked after some of them, and had written her an early Christmas letter all about them, and Jenny had been thrilled. It had been like a new, exciting story, giving her a peep into a world she knew nothing about, a world where children like herself went about in rags, and earned their own living, and slept by themselves out of doors— a world where little babies got ill because they had not enough to eat. Jenny adored babies, but the only babies she had ever met at close quarters were heavily defended by nurses in uniform, and she had not been allowed to hold them in her arms as she had longed to do. These other babies were probably too poor to have nurses, and there was a chance that she would be allowed to pick them up.

For the wonderful thing was that in a very short time

Jenny would actually see the children that Auntie Rosemary had written about; only six weeks after Christmas she and her father and mother were to set out by car on the long journey that would finish up with a visit to Auntie Rosemary and her beggar-children in the mountains of North Africa.

They were setting out in search of sunshine, for the doctor had said that Jenny needed sunshine—and therefore sunshine she must have. Tonics, medicine, cream, drives in the car—all these she had had in plenty; but neither love nor money could procure sunshine in England in January, so southward they were going to a land of blue skies and yellow beaches and calm seas, where she would grow strong and brown and sturdy. To Jenny it seemed a magic journey.

She wondered how her father would know the way, and supposed they would just follow the sun, as the Wise Men had followed the star. She was feeling rather sleepy and had quite forgotten about the A.A. and road maps. Stars, sunshine, Christmas trees—they all merged into a golden dream, and when her mother returned with the drink and sugar biscuits on a tray decorated with mistletoe she found her little daughter fast asleep. She stood looking down on the flushed face and tumbled hair for a moment, and then put out the light, opened the big window, and slipped away, leaving Jenny to dream, and to breathe in quiet healing draughts of fresh air and starry winds.

14

VERY early one morning in March, the English nurse
woke, got out of bed at once, and ran up to her flat roof
to look at the weather. It was going to be a fine day, she
decided, for the eastern sky was fleeced all over with
feathery, pink sunrise clouds, and the west was clear as
crystal. And this was just as it should be, thought the
nurse happily to herself, for this was the day she had looked
forward to for so long. Her cousin from England, with
whom she had lived as a child, was arriving to stay in the
hotel for a fortnight. Her husband was coming with her,
and they were bringing Jenny.

It was the thought of Jenny that made the English nurse
sing as she got breakfast and woke Kinza, who was lying
in a ball on a mattress on the floor, her ginger kitten close
beside her. Kinza's first action on waking was always to
stretch out her hand and make sure that the ginger kitten
was where it should be, and if by any chance it had gone
for a walk a commotion followed. But this morning all
was well, and she sat up, drew her pet into her lap, and
began to sing, too—loudly, tunelessly and timelessly; it was
her way of announcing that she was ready to be washed
and dressed in preparation for another happy day.

The English nurse, hearing the signal, came down from
the roof and attended to Kinza. Then hand in hand they
climbed the stairs again and set themselves breakfast at
a low, round table under a blue Spring sky. The nurse
sat on a stool, and Kinza and the kitten sat on a mat. The
coffee was fragrant and piping hot, the kitten's milk was
creamy, and each was perfectly satisfied with the present
company. A happier trio could not have been found anywhere, and as Kinza buried her face in her bowl the sun

came up over the roof gable and shone warm on her curls.

"The little girl is coming today," announced the nurse, as she tidied up and did her best not to trip over Kinza and the kitten, who were having a complicated game with a ball, and kept landing between her feet. "We are going to take a holiday. We will go to the market together and buy nice things to eat, and then we'll make a feast for the little girl."

"A feast, a feast!" shouted Kinza, capering about like a clumsy little kid, and falling over the waste-paper basket. "I will carry the basket for you. Let's go now."

"Yes, let's," said the nurse, and off they went into the sunshine hand in hand. She had not taken a weekday holiday for a long time; she usually stayed in in the morning. But today she had told the people not to come; she was going to be free to make ready for Jenny, and now while the day was still fresh and young she was going to climb up to the hillside behind the town and pick flowers.

It was too far for Kinza, so when they had done their shopping she left baby and basket on the step of the doughnut shop in the charge of Hamid. She often did this when she was busy, for she felt quite sure that the two children were connected—probably brother and sister —and had a right to each other's company. Kinza was always perfectly safe and happy when Hamid looked after her, although she sometimes ended up a little greasy, and not very keen on her dinner. She was very fond of doughnuts, and would eat all that were offered her.

Once by herself, the nurse almost ran up the steep, cobbled streets, past the tumbledown shacks on the outskirts of the town, with their evil-smelling rubbish-heaps, and out through the gate in the ruined wall that led on to the hillside.

She suddenly forgot she would soon be middle-aged and felt very young indeed. Singing for joy she jumped down from the rock on which she was standing and began picking flowers. They were growing all round her, for it was high tide of spring, and she gathered fragrant white narcissi, small blue irises and crimson lilies. "How beautiful they are!" she cried aloud. "I shall bring Jenny up here, and we'll pick them together."

Her thoughts went back to Jenny, and she began to feel some misgivings. Jenny was the daughter of Elizabeth, the cousin whose company had so cheered her lonely orphaned childhood, but she and her cousin had drifted apart since they had grown up. Their fortunes, their tastes, their interests were so different. Their love for Jenny seemed the only link left between them.

They had been like sisters once, but Elizabeth had married a rich man, and had gone to live in his beautiful home; here Jenny had been brought up, surrounded by beauty and peace, possessing all that love and money could give. They would gladly have made a home for Aunt Rosemary, too, but she, during her hospital training, had also come face to face with One who loved her, and He had sent her out to the little town in the mountains to seek for His lost sheep and lambs. The whole affair had seemed quite foolish to Elizabeth and her husband.

Knowing how mad it seemed to them, Rosemary had found it difficult to write about the little joys and sorrows of her lonely mission station, just as Elizabeth found it difficult to write about the happy fullness of her married life; so their occasional letters were chiefly about Jenny, and every Christmas Rosemary received a new photograph. She had kept them all in a little album, starting with a bald, round-eyed baby, who within a year had turned into a toddler in woolly leggings, staggering along with curls tumbling over her eyes. Then came Jenny in rompers on the beach, Jenny waist-high in a field of daisies, Jenny in an apron bathing her dolls. After that the years seemed to fly, and Rosemary got quite a shock one Christmas when she received a photograph of Jenny with her curls tied neatly back with a ribbon, setting off to school in a blazer and gym tunic.

The last one of all showed Jenny in full riding-kit, mounted on a pony, and it was the thought of a pony that produced the misgivings in Aunt Rosemary's mind. How foolish it was of her to build such high hopes on the child's visit! What had she to offer a little girl who had been used to riding a pony on her father's estate, and who was the owner of a dream-nursery, where china dolls as big as babies lay in proper cots under satin eider-downs? Jenny had once told her about them in a letter. She would probably be bored with the little entertain-ments that sent Moorish children into raptures. Aunt Rosemary, feeling a little downcast, hurried back down the mountain with her flowers, collected a happy, sticky Kinza, and went home.

She went to the toy-cupboard and inspected it rather sadly. There were some thumbed, dog-eared scrap-books, some faded puzzles and chipped bricks, some common little dolls and a box of stubby chalks. All had been so obviously used and loved and kissed and clutched and exulted over by children who had never seen toys before, and they were all so shabby. Aunt Rosemary shut the cupboard with a sigh, and went to the kitchen to make buns.

By half-past four the little house was as bright as scrub-bing and polishing could make it, and the sitting room was sweet with the scent of wild narcissi. Tea was laid ready, the kettle was singing on the stove, and Aunt Rosemary and Kinza went forth once more to meet the car in front of the hotel.

It arrived punctually, a smart, streamlined vehicle, and the little boys surged round, fighting each other in their efforts to carry in the luggage. Aunt Rosemary stood waiting for them to alight, and above the pandemonium she heard a clear child's voice cry out, "Oh, Mummy, look! what a sweet little girl! you never told me Aunt Rosemary had a little girl."

And then next moment they had extricated themselves

from the mob of little boys, and Elizabeth, looking just as young as she had looked ten years before, was kissing her cousin warmly. Jenny, a child of one idea, was squatting on the ground, trying to make friends with Kinza.

"Jenny," said her mother, reprovingly, "you haven't greeted Auntie Rosemary."

Jenny got up, kissed her aunt politely and turned her attention back to Kinza. The two women left them for a moment, in order to talk to Jenny's father, who was arranging about the luggage and the hotel, and, while passports were produced and forms filled in, Aunt Rosemary stood quietly watching the child, whom for ten whole years she had longed to see.

She saw a slender, long-legged little girl in a beautiful blue smocked dress and white sandals; bright hair curling loosely to her shoulders, and big grey eyes set in an eager brown face with a pointed little chin; an elfin-looking child, thought Aunt Rosemary to herself, and went over to make friends.

Jenny turned a troubled face to her aunt.

"What is the matter with this little girl?" she asked wonderingly. "I showed her my pretty brooch, and she just stares in front of her."

"I'm afraid she's blind, Jenny," said Aunt Rosemary gently. "But it doesn't mean you can't play with her. You must give her toys she can feel, and you must sing to her, and let her touch you. She'll soon love you."

She lifted Kinza's tiny hand and passed it lightly over Jenny's face and hair. "That's how she gets to know people," she explained, and then turned to speak to Mr. and Mrs. Swift, who had just arrived. But before she could say anything Jenny had seized her mother's hand and was looking up at her, her grey eyes brimming with tears.

"She's blind, Mummy," she whispered, "like the little Christmas children."

"Never mind," replied Mrs. Swift gently. "She looks a very happy little girl, and we must find her a little present. Now let's come and see Aunt Rosemary's house."

They set off across the market, the grown-ups walking ahead, and Jenny leading Kinza, too taken up with her new playmate to notice much of the town about her. She was happier than she had been all the holiday, for, much as she loved her mother and father, she was only ten, and she longed for other children to play with; most of all she longed for something to look after. She was too old for dolls; her pets had all been left at home, and she missed them dreadfully. But a curly-haired blind baby of three was far better than pets; she had never dreamed of anything so exciting.

They had reached the narrow back-street where Auntie Rosemary lived, and Mrs. Swift was talking in rather a strained voice, and trying not to look horrified at the babies sitting on the cobbles, and the ragged old beggar chanting in one of the doorways. Then she suddenly looked very horrified indeed, for Auntie Rosemary had stopped in front of the last house, and was drawing out her key; on the doorstep, barring the entrance, sat a very poor woman holding something to her breast, under her rags.

Rosemary spoke to the woman, who drew aside her rags and held out a baby, all skin and bones, half-dead with sickness and exhaustion. Mrs. Swift put out her hand to take hold of Jenny, but she was too late; her child had stepped forward, and both she and Aunt Rosemary were stooping over the pathetic little creature, quite absorbed.

"Jenny!" commanded her mother, "come here." But Jenny took not the slightest notice. She turned tragic eyes to her aunt.

"Is it going to die?" she whispered.

"I don't know; I hope not," replied Aunt Rosemary. "Let's come in."

She opened the front door, led the woman into the dispensary, and told her to sit down while she turned back to her guests. Mrs. Swift was standing very still, almost as though she had forgotten where she was, for, having got over her first shock of horror at finding such a wretched creature on Rosemary's doorstep, she had not noticed the woman's face—a young, patient face, resigned to suffering, with beautiful dark eyes that gleamed with hope as she lifted her baby towards the nurse.

"Rosemary," she urged, "don't mind about us; we can look after ourselves. You go and see to that poor baby."

Aunt Rosemary hesitated. "Well, come upstairs," she said, "and I can show you where the sitting-room is. Tea is all ready, and the kettle is boiling."

It was a surprise to enter a house in that dingy street and find it bright with pictures and flowers, and a delicious meal set out on pretty china. Aunt Rosemary, after taking them to her bedroom, sat them down on the low mattress seats, and made tea. Then she spoke rather shyly.

"It seems awfully rude," she said, "but would you mind if I left you just for ten minutes? You see, I know this woman; she's lost four babies—this one is all she's got."

Jenny slipped her hand into her aunt's.

"I'm coming to help you," she announced.

"No, Jenny," exclaimed her mother firmly; "it's quite out of the question. Come and sit down and eat your tea."

Jenny flew into a passion at once.

"I want to go!" she stormed; "I want to see that baby get well. I don't want any tea! Say I can come, Aunt Rosemary; it's your house. Daddy, say I can go. Mummy, you might let me . . ."

Her father most unexpectedly came to Jenny's rescue.

"What is the matter with that baby?" he asked. "Has it got anything infectious?"

"I shouldn't think so," answered Aunt Rosemary. "I've

seen it before; it's suffering from starvation and wrong feeding."

"Then, Elizabeth, I should let her go, if Rosemary doesn't mind," said Mr. Swift; and, as Jenny left the room triumphantly, he turned to his wife.

"Darling," he said, "let her help all she can. She needs to help someone. It may make her less self-centred to see that sort of thing, and I'm sure Rosemary will be sensible about infection."

"Perhaps so," agreed Jenny's mother, and she gave a little sigh. "If only she could have had younger brothers and sisters," she added wistfully.

Meanwhile Jenny and her aunt were bending over the white-faced baby, and the mother was recounting its pitiful history—the usual tale of poverty, ignorance, and wrong feeding. It seemed almost too late to help, but perhaps there was still a chance. Aunt Rosemary, nursing the tiny thing in the dispensary blanket, turned to Jenny.

"Go upstairs, Jenny," she said, "and bring me a cup and a spoon and some sugar from the shelf above the stove."

Jenny obeyed, moving swiftly and lightly.

"And now go and fetch the kettle," commanded her aunt.

Jenny was off in a flash.

"Now bring me those white tablets on the third shelf over there," went on her aunt, speaking very gravely; and Jenny began to feel rather uncomfortable. She was used to being admired by everyone, but she had an uncomfortable feeling that her aunt thoroughly disapproved of her.

"Now, please, rinse out the cup and spoon with some of that boiled water . . . now crush up one tablet . . . mix it with a very little water . . . pass me that bottle . . ."

Jenny forgot her temper, forgot her aunt, and forgot herself. She knelt perfectly still on the mat, only conscious of the weak little gurgling sound as the baby tried to swallow. Almost drop by drop the medicine disappeared and the baby was not sick. It took a few more spoonfuls of sweetened water, and then Aunt Rosemary began talking to the mother in Arabic, explaining that she must sit quietly for an hour and then they would give the child another drink.

"It must get better," murmured Jenny to herself. "It must! it must!"

And then Aunt Rosemary did something that surprised Jenny, who had never seen anyone do such a thing before, except in church. She pointed to the picture on the wall, of Jesus holding a child in His arms, and told the woman all about it, and then laying her hand on the woman's knees she prayed aloud for the little sick baby. Jenny could not understand what her aunt was saying, but she knew she was praying, because her eyes were closed.

"I wonder if that really does any good," thought Jenny to herself, and she too glanced up at the painting on the wall, and somehow the sight of the pictured child, so closely held, made the real baby seem safer.

"It's sure to get better," breathed Jenny to herself, bending over it again. And as she watched, the blue-veined eyelids fluttered, and the baby opened its eyes.

15

AFTER that, no further plans were needed, for Jenny announced firmly that they were going to remain in the town until it was time to go home to England and she was going to be Kinza's nurse and help Aunt Rosemary every day with the sick babies in the dispensary.

Mr. Swift laughed comfortably and then wondered what he was going to do with himself, stuck fast in an out-of-the-way mountain village for three weeks, in order to satisfy his daughter's sudden liking for sick babies. Mrs. Swift sighed anxiously and insisted that Jenny should gargle three times a day. Jenny herself was openly thrilled, and Aunt Rosemary was secretly very happy. From their point of view the holiday was being a complete success.

It was Sunday afternoon, and on Sunday no one came to the dispensary. There had been a meeting for women in the afternoon. Jenny had arrived just as they were leaving, and had watched them go slowly down the street, their babies tied tightly on their backs, and the white outer garment that covered them from head to toe thrown on top.

"They look like camels with humps, carrying their babies like that," remarked Jenny, entering the house with a hop and skip. "You'd think their babies would be suffocated, wouldn't you? Why don't they have prams like ordinary people?"

"They couldn't afford to buy them," replied Aunt Rosemary, smiling, "but it certainly isn't a very good way to carry them. A lot of the babies grow up with weak chests through lack of fresh air. You've noticed how pale some of them look."

"And spotty and thin and dirty," added Jenny wrinkling her small nose. "It's a pity there aren't more people like you to teach them how to look after their babies properly. You know, Auntie, I've been thinking, and I've decided that when I grow up I'm going to be a missionary, too, and I'm going to come out here, and have a dispensary and make all the ill people better like you do. I think it's such fun."

Aunt Rosemary looked down into the brown, confident little face lifted to hers, and she didn't answer for a moment or two.

"You couldn't be a missionary unless a very important thing happened to you first, Jenny," she said at last.

"Why not, Auntie?" enquired Jenny, surprised. "I could learn to be a nurse and how to look after babies. I wouldn't need to know anything else, would I?"

"Yes, I think you would," replied Aunt Rosemary with a little smile, "but I'm not going to tell you just here in the passage. Let's take a flask and some sandwiches, and go and have tea in the tower gardens, and then we can talk about it. Kinza will be awake by now and she loves the tower gardens.

"Oo, lovely!" cried Jenny and pranced up the stairs two steps at a time to make preparations. "Mummy said I could stay to tea if you happened to invite me. I specially asked her."

"That was very foreseeing of you," said Aunt Rosemary, laughing. "Would you like to get Kinza ready while I collect the tea? The kettle will be boiling already, so we can go almost at once."

Ten minutes later Aunt Rosemary, Jenny and Kinza were making their way across the sleepy market square to the old crumbling gate in the wall of the tower. Jenny carried the tea-basket, and Kinza carried her ball. They were chattering gaily as they climbed the steps, but as they entered the retreat of the tower garden a silence fell over them, because it was so beautiful, and Kinza stood still and sniffed appreciatively. They seemed to be walled in, not by brick or stone, but by great swaying curtains of wistaria and jasmine, and the beds were bright with wallflowers and narcissi. Sunshine streamed over everything, and the silence was broken only by the busy rattle of the storks nesting, the occasional hoarse cry of the peacock, and a soft splashing in the pond where a snow-white goose was teaching seven fluffy goslings to swim.

"Don't let Kinza fall in," warned Aunt Rosemary. "You just hang on to her while I spread out the tea."

She unpacked the basket and then sat for a few moments quietly watching the two children at play. Kinza was growing into a beautiful little girl now, strong and sturdy, with rounded limbs and soft dark curls. Who was she, and what would become of her? It was time some practical plan was made about her future, thought Aunt Rosemary to herself, if she was to grow up useful and clever with her hands. And Jenny, was she going to grow up careless, self-centred, self-satisfied?

Jenny caught sight of the spread tea and, taking Kinza's hand in hers, came running up. They were sitting on a low wall by the pond in the very centre of the garden, beneath an arch covered with little green shoots that would soon break out into a mass of rambler roses. Kinza was instantly absorbed in a bun, and Jenny, having helped herself to a sandwich, turned her questioning face to her aunt.

"What else would I have to know to be a missionary?" she asked, as though the conversation had never left off.

"It depends on what you want to do," replied Aunt Rosemary steadily. "If you simply want to heal their illnesses, then you must train to be a nurse or a doctor. But most of them are so poor that they will probably get ill again very quickly, and in any case none of our bodies last very long. The part of them that really matters is the part that is going to last for ever, their real proper selves that we call their spirits. You can only really help them and make them happy by leading them to the Lord Jesus, and you can't possibly show the Lord Jesus to anyone else unless you've seen Him yourself. So it isn't really a matter of *what* you know at all, but *whom* you know."

"But you spend ever such a long time every day giving them medicine," said Jenny. "Why couldn't I just do that?"

"You could," said Aunt Rosemary. "But, you see, you don't understand why I spend a long time giving medicines, and I'm going to explain to you. All these poor people are sinful, and only Jesus can forgive them; all of them are afraid of death, and only Jesus can take away their fear; most of them are sad and tired, and only Jesus can comfort them and give them rest. And He longs to reach them with His forgiveness and His love; but because He isn't on earth any more they can't see Him or hear Him as they did in Bible days. So He enters into the hearts of people who love Him, and He uses their lips to speak, and He uses their hands to touch. And I don't just give them medicine to make them better, much as I like to cure their illnesses. I give it because I want them to see that Jesus in me cares about their pain, and wants to help them. It's no good just *talking* about the love of Jesus; they don't understand. You have got to *show* it to them by loving deeds. But the first thing you've got to be sure of is that Jesus is actually there, loving in you and through you. Otherwise it's just like taking an empty lantern out in the dark."

Jenny was silent.

"Well, how do you know if He's there or not?" she asked curiously.

"How does the light get into the empty lantern?" asked Aunt Rosemary. "It's just a matter of opening a door, and placing a candle inside. Jesus is the Light, and He wants to come in; and we, by believing, open the door and ask Him in. Then, if the glass of the lantern is clean, the light shines out clearly; but if the glass is clouded and dirty the light will be very dim. So the first thing Jesus does with His light is to show us the sins that are going to hide Him—the tempers, self-will, impatience, and disobedience. Then, if we really want Him to, He makes us clean, and His beautiful clear beams of love shine out through us; and people lost and afraid in the dark come flocking to the light. But they don't think about the lantern at all—it's the light they want. Missionaries are really very unimportant people. They are just empty lanterns. It's the light that matters."

There was another pause.

"So I suppose only very good people can be missionaries," Jenny said thoughtfully.

"It's not exactly that," said Aunt Rosemary. "Many people are very good and kind without Jesus, just as gilded lanterns shine if you put them in the sun—but in the evening the sun sets. And our own goodness unfortunately lasts only just as long as we do—until we die. The love and life and goodness of Jesus last for ever, and the person in whom that light is burning will last for ever as well. It is what is called eternal life; and, of course, it's a far better, stronger, whiter sort of goodness than the other kind. It is perfect goodness, and no one except Jesus has ever been perfectly good."

"There are Mummy and Daddy coming into the garden," exclaimed Jenny suddenly, and she jumped up and sped along the little paths towards them, bright curls flying in the warm breeze. She was rather glad to escape from this conversation, for Aunt Rosemary was saying some quite disturbing things, and Jenny did not really like being disturbed—that bit about missionaries being unimportant, for instance. She had always been by far the most important person in the small circle in which she had lived. And very right and proper too, thought Jenny, landing with a skip in her father's arms; the smile on his face and the look in her mother's eyes reassured her at once. Whatever happened, she would always be by far the most important person in the world to her mother and father.

Auntie Rosemary followed, leading a rather crumby Kinza, and her eyes met Elizabeth's over Jenny's head, happy and understanding, because it was still so wonderful to see Jenny running about and strong again. One of the best parts of the holiday to both women had been the renewal of their old friendship, which now blossomed as strong and sure as it had done before their very different ways of life had seemed to separate them. Elizabeth's charm and kindness and the serenity of her married life drew out Rosemary's admiration; and Elizabeth, on her side, had come to admit that her cousin was not altogether wasting her time. The look on the face of the sick baby's mother had taught her that, and in spite of the germs and sores of the dispensary she trusted Rosemary with Jenny as she had never trusted anyone before. And this was strange, for a few weeks ago she, who had always been so careful to surround her little girl with sunshine and beauty, would have been horrified at Jenny's having anything to do with poverty and illness.

' But there are different sorts of beauty,' she had thought to herself. ' Healing and helping and loving and giving are beautiful. I don't want Jenny to be a recluse, or anything like that. I want her to get on in the world and marry well —but I want her to grow up good and unselfish, too, and I think Rosemary can help her in that way.'

When she had voiced her thoughts to her husband he had agreed. " She's learning something practical in that dispensary," he said, " and she may find she's cut out for nursing. They don't seem to think at school that she's overburdened with brains, and if war comes later she'll have to do something like everyone else."

Whereupon Jenny's mother had shuddered and changed the subject. Jenny and war did not seem to her to fit at all; and she disliked their being mentioned in the same breath.

" Rosemary," said Elizabeth, nestling Kinza against her, " couldn't you desert your little brats just for once this evening, and come and have supper with us at the hotel?"

" They don't come on Sunday," replied Rosemary. " It's my day off, except for the afternoon meeting. I'd love to come. I'll go home and get Kinza safely to sleep, and then I'll be along."

"Oh, Mummy, look!" cried Jenny. "The peacock has opened his tail." And she hurried her parents off to see, while Rosemary and Kinza made their slow way home, the low sun sending long, bright, mellow rays across the market square.

An hour later she was sitting in the big hotel dining-room, under a cut-glass chandelier, eating a four-course dinner with Mr. and Mrs. Swift and Jenny, who had all dressed up in their very best to welcome her. It was a great treat to Rosemary to come out to supper, and there was always so much to say when she and Elizabeth got together. Tonight the talk turned upon Kinza.

"She's such a beautiful little creature," said Mrs. Swift; "it seems so cruel she should be blind. What do you propose to do with her in the future, Rosemary?"

"I would like her to go to some training school in about three years' time," said Rosemary, "where she can learn Braille and basket-work. She could earn her own living like that out here, and when she was really proficient she could come back to me. A blind girl who was a true Christian could be a missionary to her own people later on."

Jenny leaned forward across the table, nearly upsetting her glass in her eagerness.

"The Blind School, Daddy!" she cried, "where they invited us all at Christmas. If Kinza went there, Mummy, she could come and stay with us sometimes, and I'd look after her; it would be like having a little sister, and I'd see her lots and lots, and she'd be so happy if I was there; and they had such a lovely time at Christmas. Oh, when can she come, Auntie Rosemary? Couldn't we take her home with us this time?"

The cousins looked at each other questioningly.

"It's not a bad idea of Jenny's," said Mrs. Swift. "It's an awfully good school, and they take them quite young.

John could easily get her nominated free. He's on the Board, and has a lot of influence. The sooner she goes, the more quickly she'd pick up English. Also she could travel with us in the car instead of your having to bring her."

Rosemary hesitated. She just didn't know what to answer. It was all so sudden. Jenny was jumping up and down in her chair in her excitement.

"Jenny gets tired of these long car drives," added Mrs. Swift. "She's always so much happier if there's another child in the car."

"I just don't know what to say," replied Rosemary. "It's most awfully kind of you . . . but somehow she seems so wee to go away just yet . . . could I think it over and give you an answer in a day or two?"

"Of course," answered Mrs. Swift. "Just let us know when you feel sure. No, Jenny, don't go on and on about it; people can't make up their minds on important matters without a little 'think' first, or they may make them up wrongly."

"I've made mine up upon this important matter," announced Jenny dramatically. "Oh, Auntie Rosemary, I'm sure you'll say yes. It really does seem to be the best idea I've ever had in my life. Even Mummy and Daddy thought it good!— Oh, look, Daddy, there are ice-creams for pudding, the kind you don't like. Please will you pretend you'd like one, and I'll eat it for you, as well as mine."

In her excitement at the possibility of getting two ice-creams Jenny forgot about Kinza for the moment, and the talk turned to other subjects. Pleasantly the evening passed until Rosemary rose to go.

"Daddy and I will take you home," said Mrs. Swift, rising too. "Jenny, darling, run up to bed."

"All right," answered Jenny, who, having enjoyed her two ice-creams, was in an unusually obliging mood. She flung her arms round her aunt's neck, and drew her head down close to her mouth, so that no one could hear what they were saying.

"You are going to think hard about it, aren't you, Auntie?" she whispered.

"Yes, Jenny, very hard—I'm going to ask God to show me the right way, too."

"Do you think He'll have shown you by tomorrow morning?"

"I don't know, Jenny—it's such a big thing. Give me two days!"

"Well, ask Him to show you as quick as possible—and ask Him to let it be Yes."

"Couldn't you ask too?"

"I don't really know how to . . . but I'll try . . . Goodnight, Auntie Rosemary."

"Goodnight, Jenny."

She loosened the child's clinging arms gently, and set out across the dark market-place with Mr. and Mrs. Swift. Under the street lamp she turned to wave, and Jenny waved back, black against the bright background of the huge doorway.

16

HAMID welcomed the coming of spring for, however hardy you are, you never quite get used to blue toes and fingers and wet clinging rags, to bitter winds and driving rain and snow on bare chapped skin. But all that was over now; the sun shone warm and comforting, the storks nested in the towers, flowers clothed the mountain, and cherry and peach blossom made the valley beautiful. Baby goats skipped and jostled in the streets, and Hamid, like all other young, growing things, had shot up several inches and looked more like a little scarecrow than ever. The clothes that the English nurse had given him had fallen to pieces, but this no longer mattered. He stretched himself luxuriously on the step of the doughnut stall, licked the oil off his fingers, and watched the seething market with bright observant eyes.

There was always so much to see in the square on market days. The country women were streaming in, strong, weather-tanned and loud-voiced, bowed almost double under huge loads of charcoal. Then a lorry arrived, laden with boxes of silver fish fresh from the Mediterranean, and the market loafers all surged forward to earn a few coins by carrying the dripping boxes on their heads to the fish market. Grubby little boys darted in and out of the crowd trying to sell dusty dough-rings on strings, and donkeys jostled and brayed. Hamid saw Kinza in a scarlet jersey prancing along between Jenny and the English nurse who had come out to do her shopping.

Then in a flash he caught sight of something else. He thought he was dreaming for a second, and rubbed the light from his eyes and looked again. He was not dreaming. He went very white under his tan, turned a backward somersault into the shop and hid himself securely between the stone oven and the counter on which the doughnuts had sizzled earlier that morning. Then he peeped out, like a startled rabbit from its hole, to watch what would happen next.

His step-father stood rigid in a doorway opposite, staring fixedly at the little party who were unconsciously buying oranges. Then drawing a step or two nearer he watched Kinza as a snake might watch a baby rabbit at play, waiting its moment to strike. His keen eyes were taking in everything: the blind gestures, the happy freedom of her baby prattle, the stout little shoes and good warm clothes. As the three went over to the oil-merchant's he followed, coming very close to his step-daughter, so close that for one breathless moment Hamid wondered if he was going to snatch her up. But he did not touch her. He merely moved behind them, inconspicuous in the jostling crowd, and Hamid noticed that his black eyes burned with anger and his mouth was closed as tightly as a cruel, steel trap.

Hamid, recovering from his first shock, was not afraid. His father had come over to the market on business, and would doubtless leave the town that evening. He had not seen Hamid, nor would he see him, for at the earliest possible moment Hamid would run off to the mountains, and keep company with the monkeys until after dark. For Kinza he felt not the smallest anxiety. Kinza was in the safe keeping of the English nurse who loved her and would never let her go. Her home was a fortress into which his father could never penetrate. Hamid himself would remain in the burrow until his master released him, and then— over the hills and far away.

The master arrived quite soon, and was surprised and annoyed to find his assistant under the counter instead of at it. He boxed his ears, which Hamid did not mind in the least, and cut a centime off his pay, which he minded quite a lot. However, he soon forgot in the delight of his dangerous freedom, for the market lay between him and the mountain, and somewhere, swallowed up in the crowds, lurked his step-father.

He was nimble on his brown feet, however, and he crossed the danger-zone and made for the cobbled path that ran along the outskirts of the town overlooking the steep river valley below.

Kinza, Jenny, and Aunt Rosemary made their way home, and never noticed the sinister figure of the man who followed them as far as the entrance of the street and stood watching until the door of the house closed behind them. It was almost time for the dispensary to open. Usually, while Aunt Rosemary worked there, Kinza sat on the front step in the sunshine and talked to the kitten, and the patients stepped over or round her; but during the past fortnight she had often been to play with Jenny, who loved looking after her. So now, with her new story-book which she had brought to show her aunt in one hand, and Kinza holding on to the other, Jenny set off to find her mother and father at the hotel.

The two little girls threaded their way through the market crowds and entered the tower gardens which lay between them and the hotel. There was no one in the gardens, for everyone was busy buying and selling, and the sleepy silence made her want to linger. She thought of her new book; she had reached such an exciting part, and this would be a lovely quiet place to sit and read just for five minutes. Her mother had told her she was never to loiter or sit down between her aunt's house and the hotel, but, after all, her mother did not know what time she set out. There was a fascinating little stone nook under a wistaria curtain near the old archway that led into another part of the garden. She sat down with Kinza beside her and buried herself in the story.

It was a story after Jenny's own heart—about a child who had a pony of her own and rode in gymkhanas, just as Jenny was going to do when she got home. She hardly noticed that Kinza had risen to her feet and started to wander along the path towards the archway. Kinza often went for little walks, her arms held out in front of her to avert danger; when she felt she had gone far enough she would stand still and squeak till someone fetched her back.

Jenny read eagerly on, for she must reach the end of the chapter and discover whether Annabel's pony was going to win the cup for jumping or not. Out of the corner of her eye she could see Kinza standing in the archway. She must fetch her back in a minute, but she would be quite all right while Jenny just finished the page—and then just one page more.

She skimmed to the end and got up quickly with a sigh of relief, because Annabel had won easily. But she felt guilty of having let Kinza stray through the archway alone. "Kinza!" she called eagerly, running into the shadows and out into the sunshine of the other part of the garden, and then she stopped short and her eyes grew big with fright. For the green plot in front of her was empty and deserted—there was no sign of Kinza anywhere.

With her heart beating wildly she ran from bush to bush, searching behind every one; up and down the steps she flew, back into the walled garden, but it was no good; not a trace remained to tell which path the stumbling little feet had followed. Kinza had completely disappeared.

Jenny rushed out into the market, half-blind with panic, bumping into people and nearly treading on the goods set out for sale. People turned to look at her anxiously, pushing her way wildly in and out, with her pale, tear-stained cheeks and big, frightened eyes. They thought she had lost her mother, and pointed toward the hotel, but she only shook her head and rushed on, searching frantically.

At last she stood still, completely out of breath, and, because there was nowhere else to look, and because she did not like the people staring at her, she went back to the garden and stood alone by the fatal archway, trying to decide what to do next.

She simply could not go back to her aunt. Aunt Rosemary had trusted her alone with Kinza, and she had failed completely in her trust. What would her aunt say? And, worse still, where was Kinza? Had something terrible happened to her? Was she frightened or hurt and crying out, wondering why Jenny did not come to her? Jenny did not know. She burst into tears and ran sobbing to the hotel, up the stairs to her mother's room, and into her mother's arms.

It took Mrs. Swift some minutes to piece the confused story together, but when she finally succeeded in unravelling what had happened she went rather white, too. She dried Jenny's eyes, and took her by the hand.

"We must go and tell Auntie Rosemary at once," she said quietly. "We'll have one more look in the market-place on the way."

Jenny stood quite still. "I *can't* go to Aunt Rosemary," she said tragically; "I just *can't,* Mummy. You'll have to go and tell her."

"No," said Mrs. Swift, still quietly, but very firmly, "you must come and tell her yourself. You see, Jenny, this has happened because you were disobedient and untrustworthy, and you must just be brave and take the blame you deserve. And we must go now at once, because if anyone has taken Kinza every moment may matter. Daddy is on the terrace and he'll come with us."

It was a silent little party that set out from the hotel. Mr. Swift suggested that he should do one more quick search in the market-place while Jenny and her mother scoured the gardens again; and they separated at the steps. Ten minutes later they met again, grave and anxious.

"Well," said Mr. Swift, "the sooner we get Rosemary on to this the better. She can speak the language and question the people."

They met Rosemary coming across the market to look for Kinza at the hotel, as it was her dinner time. Mr.

Swift told her what had happened, and while he spoke Jenny stood a little apart, her eyes fixed on the ground, not daring to look at her aunt's face. She wondered what her aunt would say, and whether she would reproach her bitterly right there in the middle of the market. But, as it happened, nothing was said about her carelessness just then. Everyone seemed to have forgotten about it. All they were thinking about was Kinza.

They went back to the walled garden, to see the exact place so that Aunt Rosemary could question the shop keepers nearest the spot, but no one could give her any news. Whatever had happened had happened just the other side of the archway, and the archway was hidden from the road by a high wall. There were three exits from that part of the garden, and one led straight out on to a lonely country road that branched off in the next couple of miles into a dozen wild mountain tracks.

"There are two possibilities," said Aunt Rosemary at last, when all questioning had proved fruitless. "One is that she has been kidnapped for the sake of her clothes, and in that case the police might help us; the other is that her own people have decided they want her back again and have stolen her away. In that case I'm afraid she has gone for good. After all, I have no claim to her against her own people. I don't even know where she came from in the first place; I only know she was not a local child . . ." She stopped abruptly as a new thought suggested itself to her. "I wonder where Hamid is," she went on eagerly. "I've often thought he had something to do with her—he might be able to give some clue."

But not one of the crowd of boys who had collected to see what was going on could tell of Hamid's whereabouts. He had been at his post that morning, and had last been seen making for the mountains. Everyone volunteered to go and look for him, and they scattered in all directions, on twinkling brown feet, for the rich Englishman would no doubt reward the finder handsomely. But no one succeeded in tracking him to earth, for he was far up the ravine between the great rocks, throwing stones at the monkeys. And so frightened was he of meeting his step-father that he stayed there till long after sunset and missed the boys' meeting for the first time in many weeks.

The police, when they had heard the story, were courteous and sympathetic, but not very hopeful. They promised to 'phone the Government outposts in the mountains to watch the main tracks and check up on travellers, but the countless little bypaths known only to the villagers ran far outside their reach. Besides, even if the child were found, what was there to prove that she did not belong to her captors? They could be fined for stealing the clothes, but the child . . . the policeman shrugged his shoulders very expressively, lifted his eyebrows, cocked his head on one side, and spread out both hands. There was no more to be said.

Nor was there any more to be done, so they went sorrow-fully back to Aunt Rosemary's house to have some tea, as everyone had been far too busy and upset to think about dinner. But none of them felt hungry, and after a while Mr. and Mrs. Swift rose to go, and Jenny, pale and wretched, followed them, still not daring to look at her aunt, who, as a matter of fact, had hardly given her naughtiness a thought yet. She was far too taken up in wondering what had become of Kinza.

Rosemary was glad to be left alone. She carried out the tea things, and then came back into her little room and knelt down, meaning to pray for Kinza. But the kitten sprang up beside her, mewing for its little playmate, and under the cushion on which she rested her arms was some-thing hard and knobbly—Kinza's wooden doll. She gazed round the room, and there was Kinza's ball, Kinza's mat, Kinza's box of sweets that Jenny had given her. Everywhere she looked there were signs of the missing, loved little presence, and Rosemary suddenly laid down her head on her arms and her anxiety seemed to over-whelm her. Where was Kinza? and what was happening to her? How terrified and homesick she would be, how helpless in her bewildering darkness! "O God," she cried, "take care of her; don't let her be hurt or afraid; bring her back safely to me."

As she prayed, she heard a little sob behind her and realized she was not alone in the room. She looked up quickly, and there in the doorway stood Jenny, white-faced and swollen-eyed with crying.

"Jenny!" exclaimed Rosemary, surprised. "Does Mummy know you've come?"

"Yes," said Jenny with a gulp. "I said I must see you alone, so Mummy brought me back to the door, and you'd forgotten to bolt it, so I just came in, and she says please will you see me home when you've finished with me . . . and I don't suppose you want to see me at all . . . because . . . because . . . it was all my fault about Kinza, and oh, Auntie, whatever shall I do?"

The last words came out with a rush of fresh tears and Aunt Rosemary drew the trembling little girl into the room, shut the door and sat down beside her.

"You can't do anything, Jenny," she said gently, "but God loves Kinza far more than we do, and He can do everything. Let's kneel down and ask God together to shelter little Kinza and comfort her and keep her safe."

So they knelt side by side, and Aunt Rosemary committed Kinza to the arms of the Good Shepherd. Jenny listened and wondered, more miserable than she had ever been before. It was all very well for Aunt Rosemary, she thought to herself. When dreadful things happened to Aunt Rosemary she had a place of refuge—a place where in any time of need she could find forgiveness and peace and comfort. But Jenny knew no such refuge. She felt shut out in the dark. She would never forgive herself, and neither would anyone else, if Kinza were really lost.

For the first time in her life her naughtiness had really mattered, and there seemed no escape from the terrible results of it. Nearly every day she was self-willed and would have her own way and lost her temper if thwarted, but Mummy and Daddy were always nice and understanding about it, and remembered that after all she had been ill for three months. Now she had gone her own way and disobeyed once too often.

"If only Kinza could come back," said Jenny to herself, "I would never be disobedient or naughty again. I'd be good for ever and ever."

17

ROSEMARY spent most of next day trying to trace Hamid, but Hamid was apparently determined not to be traced, and, on hearing early in the morning that he was urgently wanted by the English nurse, he cut work and made straight for the mountains. Why should the English nurse want him urgently just then? Perhaps his father had spoken to her and she was going to hand him over. It was all most suspicious and Hamid decided to keep clear of her.

However, the English nurse was so very much in earnest that on being told that Hamid had gone up into the mountains early she cancelled her boys' meeting and settled herself just before sunset behind the pillar of the great stone archway through which he was likely to return. She did not have to wait very long. Before the light had faded over the western ranges a weary little figure skulked in through the shadows and the English nurse grabbed hold of him by what remained of his shirt.

For a moment he struggled violently, but she spoke to him at once, and her words arrested him, so that he stood still. "Hamid," she was saying pleadingly, "I've lost Kinza. Please can you help me to find her again? Do you know where she might have gone to?"

She kept tight hold of him and he stood rigidly in front of her, gazing up at her uncertainly. At first he was too startled to collect his thoughts, but gradually his mind cleared, and he began to put two and two together. If Kinza had disappeared, her father had certainly taken her home, and if the nurse was searching for her, then she certainly did not know about their father. But it did not seem safe to tell: it might lead to contact with the police, and no little outlaw boy ever wishes to have anything to do with the police; or it might lead to meeting his people—or it might all be a trick or a trap. It was far safer to deny all knowledge and have nothing to do with it.

And yet if he refused to speak, Kinza was lost, and all his efforts were wasted; and Kinza had been so happy, so fat, so safe. Now she would be sold to the beggar—why else should his father want her?—and he would not be there to protect her.

"I don't know anything about it," he said warily, after a long pause, but his eyes, by the light of the archway lamp, were bright and starry with unshed tears at the thought of Kinza, and the nurse, seeing them and noting the pause, felt quite sure that he knew a great deal about it —though it might be very difficult to worm it out of him, and she must proceed with the utmost tact and care.

"Let's go home and have some supper together," she said soothingly, "and we can talk about it in the house. You must be hungry after being on the mountain all day."

He had shared a piece of rye bread with a shepherd boy at midday, but apart from that he had had nothing to eat since the evening before, having forfeited his work and his wages, and he was ravenously, wolfishly hungry. There was a gnawing pain inside him, and unless he accepted the English nurse's offer there was very little hope of food that night. It was rather rash to go to her house, because after all it might be a trick, but nobody could make him talk. His hunger overcame his caution. He slipped a dirty little hand into the hand of the English nurse, and she clasped it firmly and let go the scruff of his neck. She did not let go his hand until they were safely inside the house with the door locked behind them.

She led Hamid upstairs to the room where he had once seen Kinza asleep, and he sat down cross-legged on the mat, tense with excitement, and sniffed rapturously, for the pot was on the fire, and the house was full of the fragrant odour of hot rice and vegetables cooked in olive oil. She brought him a steaming bowlful and a great hunk of bread, and then fetched her own and sat down on the mattress near him. She did not question him while he ate, for he was completely absorbed in his food, but she watched him thoughtfully. He was extraordinarily like Kinza in looks—the same dark bright eyes set widely apart under a broad forehead; the same heart-shaped face, the broad cheek-bones tapering to a beautifully moulded little chin, and the same determined mouth. She waited until the last delicious drop of food had gone, and the bowl wiped clean with a crust of bread, and then she spoke with a certainty that she did not feel.

"Hamid," she said very firmly, "do you know who has stolen away your little sister Kinza? If you know, you must tell me, because I want to get her back again."

The English nurse was very tired, very strained, very afraid that her guess was wrong. Her voice, which had been so firm, quivered a little as she finished speaking, and that quiver reassured Hamid. This was no trick, no scheme to catch him out. It was the honest cry of a loving heart, and Hamid wriggled closer, and squatted with his head close to her knees, his flushed face upturned to hers. "I think my step-father has got her," he replied. "I saw him watching her in the market yesterday. He followed her right across the Square, but I thought she was safe with you."

If the nurse was startled by her success she did not show it. Any false move might scare him into silence. She went on speaking very quietly.

"Where does your step-father live?"

Hamid told her the name of the village.

"Did he not know she was with me?"

"No."

The English nurse made another guess.

"Why did you put her in my passage that night?"

"My mother told me to."

"Why?"

" My father did not want Kinza. He was going to sell her to a beggar. Kinza would have been very unhappy, so my mother sent her to you."

" And now?"

" My father will sell her to the beggar. He wants the money."

The nurse shuddered. Kinza's prospects were far worse than she had even imagined, and she must save her somehow. She went on quietly questioning:

" How far is the village?"

" Two days' journey on a horse—but my father probably came by road on a market lorry. That only takes about six hours."

" And you—how did you come?"

" Partly on a lorry—mostly walking."

" And Kinza?"

" On my back."

He spoke in the tones he would have used had he been speaking of a walk up the street, and the nurse marvelled at his courage; surely he, who had dared so much for Kinza's sake, would help her now!

" And if I went to your village, and offered to pay your father more than the beggar, would he let me buy back Kinza?"

" I don't know; he might. But how would you know the house? There are many parts of the village with hills between."

" You must come with me and show me."

" I can't. My father would beat me dreadfully if I went home."

" You need not come home. You can point out the house from a distance."

" But everyone in the village knows me. They will tell my father."

" We will arrive after sunset in the car of the Englishman. No one will see you in the dark. Surely you will do this to save Kinza!"

She had leaned forward in her earnestness and laid her hands on his shoulders, and he sat there scratching his head doubtfully, battling with his fears.

"Hamid," she pleaded, "if you refuse I shan't be able to find her. The beggar will have her, and she will suffer and be cold and hungry in the streets of a big city, and all her life she'll live in the dark. If she comes back to me she will be happy, and I will teach her about the Lord Jesus, and she'll grow up with her heart full of light and happiness—I've told you about Him so many times, Hamid. Do you believe in Him yet?"

He glanced up at her, his face bright with shy love.

"I love the Lord Jesus very much," he replied simply. "He has taken my sins away, and He has made my heart happy."

The nurse caught at his words eagerly.

"Then He can also take your fears away and make your heart brave," she urged. "It says in God's Book that the perfect love of Jesus in our hearts casts out our fear. There isn't any more room for it. Let's ask Him now, Hamid, to cast out your fear and to save Kinza."

He shut his eyes obediently, held out his cupped hands as though to receive some poured-out blessing, and as the nurse prayed he repeated the words after her, and made them his own. While he was speaking two thoughts came into his mind: if the Lord Jesus really loved him He would not let his father beat him, and therefore there was nothing to be afraid of; and what fun it would be to drive all the way to his village in the Englishman's big, fast, grey car.

So even while he prayed, the Spirit of God breathed happy, brave thoughts into his troubled heart, so when they had finished praying he was quite ready to agree to the nurse's suggestions, and finally left the house in a state of pleasant excitement. As he wandered across the market place he saw himself sitting upright at the car window, waving proudly, and his friends, green with envy, watching his royal progress spellbound. He suddenly chuckled with glee and skipped in the air. The warm night breezes fanned his hot cheeks, and he thrilled to the adventure. About the final result he had no doubt at all. His father would do anything for money, and the nurse would certainly offer more than the beggar would give.

As soon as he had left the house, Rosemary set off for the hotel to lay her plan before Mr. and Mrs. Swift. She had not seen them since early morning, when they had been round to say that Jenny seemed so restless and upset that they had decided to go for a long motor drive into the mountains and take a picnic dinner. Jenny, full of impossible plans for rescuing Kinza, had not wished to go at all, but her father had insisted. There had been rather a scene in consequence, and they had driven off with Jenny looking like a sulky thundercloud, hunched up in the back of the car.

She found them sitting in the lounge looking tired and depressed. They had been to her house earlier to inquire if there was any news, but she had been up at the Gate watching for Hamid. They jumped up at the sight of her.

"Has anything happened?" they asked eagerly.

"Yes," said Rosemary, unable to hide her excitement. She dropped into an empty chair, and leaning forward she poured out the wonderful story.

"Of course, I've gone and fixed it all up with Hamid without consulting you," she ended, "but I felt quite, quite sure you'd be willing, because you've been so sweet about Kinza. We would have to start tomorrow afternoon—it's about four hours' drive—in order to arrive soon after sunset. Then Hamid says it's a good walk on beyond where the car can go. We should not be back till the small hours of the morning, but I didn't think you'd mind that for once."

"Of course not," Mrs. Swift assured her, as eager as she was. "John shall take you and Hamid, and I'll stay with Jenny. I don't think she ought to go. I know she could sleep in the car, but it means rousing her in the middle of the night when we get home."

"There'll be no end of a rumpus if she's left behind," said her father, and the eagerness vanished from their faces and they both sighed.

"Is Jenny in bed?" enquired Rosemary. "Could I tell her all about it, or will she be asleep?"

Mr. and Mrs. Swift glanced at each other, and there was a moment's silence. Then Mrs. Swift spoke.

"Yes, do go and tell her," she said, "and, Rosemary, I wish you could somehow talk her into a better frame of mind. She's so fond of you, and I don't seem able to do anything with her tonight. We've had such a miserable day. She sulked and grumbled from the moment we set out till the moment we got home—because she didn't want to come at all. She wanted to stay and help you look for Kinza. Of course, I know she's been ill and all that, but really she does behave like a spoilt baby when she can't get her own way."

"So I sent her to bed when we got in," added Mr. Swift gloomily. "Her tempers are getting too much of a good thing. She's not used to being punished and took it very badly, so I don't know what sort of a mood you'll find her in, poor little girl. She'll certainly kick up an awful fuss if she's not allowed to go tomorrow."

"Poor Jenny!" said Aunt Rosemary. "I'll go and see if she's still awake," and she climbed the stairs rather slowly and knocked at the door. There was no answer. She opened the door and went in.

"What do you want?" said a sullen voice from under the bedclothes. "I haven't gone to sleep early like you said, so you needn't think I have."

"It's me, Jenny," said Aunt Rosemary quietly, and went over and sat down on the bed.

Jenny came out at once, rather embarrassed, for she always spoke politely in front of Aunt Rosemary, wishing to keep up the picture of herself as a pleasant child. However, Mummy and Daddy had probably been telling about her, and she must make Auntie Rosemary see her point of view. Mummy and Daddy completely misunderstood her and were cross with her when they should have been sorry for her, but surely her aunt would understand and be nice and see how ill-used she was.

"Oh, Auntie Rosemary," cried Jenny bursting into tears; "I'm so glad you've come! I've been thinking about Kinza all day long."

"Oh, no, you haven't," replied Aunt Rosemary in a very matter-of-fact voice. "You've been thinking about yourself all day long, and that's why you are so unhappy. Selfish people are always unhappy because they mind so much when they can't have their own way."

"I'm *not* selfish," sobbed Jenny angrily. "You don't understand any more than Mummy and Daddy do. I couldn't stop wondering where Kinza was, and they took me right away where I couldn't find out or hear if there was any news."

"But your hearing the news wouldn't have helped Kinza at all," replied Aunt Rosemary. "It would just have satisfied your own curiosity. And because you couldn't be satisfied you made Mummy and Daddy miserable all day long, and if that's not selfish I don't know what is."

Jenny could think of nothing to say to that, so she merely repeated forlornly, "You don't understand."

"Oh, Jenny, Jenny, I understand so well," cried Aunt Rosemary, suddenly kneeling down and drawing the angry, hot little girl towards her. "I understand that because you have always had everything you want, and because Mummy and Daddy have always given you such lovely things, and been so good to you, you think nothing matters in the world except your own happiness. Your heart is like a little closed-in circle with yourself in the middle, and every time anything happens that hurts or annoys you, you think the world is coming to an end. And as you get older, Jenny, you will find that there are more and more things that will annoy and hurt you, and you are going to grow up into such a very unhappy, un-loving woman. You see, you haven't really time or room to love anyone else properly because all your love is being poured in on yourself."

Jenny was quite silent. No one had ever talked to her like this before. Her mother and father usually ended these affairs by saying, " Never mind, darling; we're sure you didn't mean it. Let's forget all about it."

But perhaps Auntie Rosemary was partly speaking the truth. It was worrying to remember how often she felt very, very unhappy, simply because it was not always possible for her to have her own way. How lovely it would be to be the sort of person who was always happy and who did not seem to mind very much if she couldn't have what she wanted! There was a girl at school, for instance, who had wanted to learn riding, and who had wanted a new dress for the party, but she couldn't have either because her father couldn't afford it. Yet she had kept quite calm about it and had seemed to enjoy the party hugely in a cast-off dress of her sister's. Jenny could not understand it, and decided she was simply made differently.

" I can't help minding things," said Jenny at last, in a small aggrieved voice. " And I do love people. I love Mummy and Daddy and you and Kinza and lots of people."

" Only as long as we please you," replied Aunt Rose-mary. " Directly we stop doing what you want you are quite happy to make us miserable, as you've made Mummy and Daddy miserable today."

Jenny was silent again, but she had drawn very close to the kneeling figure beside her. It was no good trying to go on making Auntie Rosemary admire her, because apparently she knew all about her, and in that knowledge there was a curious kind of peace. Jenny suddenly felt she could drop all pretences and utter what is the real deep-down but sometimes unrecognized longing of every child's heart.

" I do want to be good and happy," she whispered, " and

I *do* want to make Mummy happy. But I can't. I just seem to mind things so much that I can't help being cross."

"Yes," agreed Aunt Rosemary thoughtfully, "I know. Our own selves with all their wantings and mindings are very, very difficult to move out of the centre of the circle. In fact, I know only one way to do it. That is to ask the Lord Jesus to come into the circle with His wishes and to turn out your self. At first it's not easy because your self keeps wanting things as well, and you have to keep saying, 'Not my will, but Yours.' But after a time a wonderful thing happens. As we learn to know the Lord Jesus, and talk to Him, and as He talks to us, we gradually come to love Him so much that His wishes become our wishes, and we begin to want only the things He wants. It says in the Bible that when we want the same thing as the Lord Jesus, we only have to ask for it and we get it. Then of course we are perfectly satisfied, happy people."

"I don't see how you mean," whispered Jenny sorrowfully.

"No," agreed Aunt Rosemary. "It does sound rather difficult, doesn't it? But it is really quite simple if you think of it like this. It all starts by asking the Lord Jesus to forgive us and to turn out our selfishness, and to come in and live in the centre of our lives instead. When He comes we shall start loving Him, because He loves us so much. When you love people you want to look at them and get near to them. When you look at Jesus and come near to Him, you grow like Him, and you want what He wants. It's like looking at something very bright, and reflecting the light so that you look bright yourself."

"Oh, I see," said Jenny, rather sleepily. She had stopped crying and was lying very still. Aunt Rosemary waited a moment and then said, "I really came to tell you some news of Kinza. We've discovered where she's gone, and tomorrow your father and Hamid and I are going to her home, and we are going to try to persuade her father to let us have her back."

"Oh, where? when? how?" cried Jenny, springing up

in bed. "Tell me all about it quick! Can I come, too?"

"No," said Aunt Rosemary, "you can't. Mummy says it's too late, and probably in a native village the fewer of us the better. You've got a good chance to make up for today by obeying without any sulking or crossness. Now I'll tell you how I found out, and all about it," and as she told it, Jenny lay and listened in an unusually humble frame of mind.

It was all going to come right after all, perhaps, and she did not deserve it. Last night she had made a sort of promise—"If Kinza comes back I'm going to be good for ever and ever."

"Auntie," she whispered penitently, her face half-buried in the pillow, "tell Mummy to come. I want to tell her I'm sorry, and I want to tell her I'll be good tomorrow."

18

THE next day dawned bright and clear, and the rescue party set off early in the afternoon. Jenny, desperately disappointed that she was not going too, but determined to make the best of it, stood in the middle of the sunlit market-place and waved them off. Hamid, all his fears forgotten in the thrill of being inside the beautiful car, sat like some small royal personage in the back seat and nodded condescendingly to the crowd of open-mouthed, admiring urchins running behind. Far down the road they followed, shouting and hooting, bare feet twinkling, rags fluttering, until the car gathered speed and raced away from them. Hamid stuck his cropped head far out of the window and yelled with triumph, and Rosemary pulled him in again by the seat of his trousers.

It was a beautiful drive. Hamid remembered the hot dusty evening when he had toiled up the same white hill, with Kinza on his back. He had been too tired then to look about him and admire the view, but now he was anxious to see all there was to see, and he leapt from side to side of the car like a tame monkey in a cage. Everywhere he looked he could see sloping fields of young wheat, or bright banks of flowers. Little streams rushed under the road and foamed downhill to meet the river—a blue strip in the valley below them winding between the oleanders.

They reached the level river-road in the valley, and the car sped along between low hillocks starred with bushes of white flowers. The golden air was heavy with their fragrance, and Hamid, suddenly tired by his exertions curled up on the seat and fell fast asleep. He slept for some time, and when he woke the car had stopped on the crest of a hill. Wherever you looked, backward, forward, to left or right, you could see mountains. The Englishman and the nurse were drinking tea out of a thermos flask, and eating sandwiches. Hamid stuck his head over the back of the seat to show he was awake, and was given a big round bun with sugar on top; and as he settled himself among the leather cushions, and licked the sugar off first, he wondered whether Heaven could hold any improvements.

Only one thought dimmed his pleasure. As the sun sank towards the western mountains the grey car was travelling toward his village and his father. The big Englishman and the nurse had promised that he should be kept safe, so he was not really very afraid. Only it was a sobering thought, and he laid his head on his arms on the window-ledge and pondered it in silence. He was drawing near to his mother, too, and his heart cried out for her. It would be hard to be so near and yet unable to see her or speak to her. Two big tears brimmed up in his eyes and trickled over on to the shiny leather.

The car swung off into a main road, leaving a town on the right. They were heading straight for the city, and big cars whizzed past them, as magnificent as their own. Hamid forgot his sorrows temporarily and began careering from side to side again, thrilled by the gleaming bonnets and flashing windscreens. If only they were going right on to the city by the sea where great ships lay at anchor in the harbour! But they were not; for after a short while they turned aside up a mountain road and travelled on between scrubby hills where the villages of the tribes-people nestled, straw-thatched in the hollows.

Behind these hills the sun set in a glory of blinding light. Children were bringing their goats home, and several times the car had to stop while a small lithe figure and its flock, black against the orange west, crossed the road. Then the light faded and dusk fell, and Hamid could see the shape of his own home mountain in the distance with two bright stars twinkling above it. His heart began to beat very fast and his mouth felt rather dry. But the car was travelling slowly because of the stony country road, jolting them in their seats.

It was quite dark when they reached the well-known market-place, with its rustling eucalyptus trees and the government buildings white in the moonlight. They drove on unchallenged beyond the few native shops to where the rough road dwindled into a track, and there Mr. Swift brought the car to a standstill.

Hamid tumbled out and ran behind an olive tree while the nurse spoke to a boy standing in the doorway of a house, and asked him to mind the car. He knew this boy, and did not wish to be recognized by anyone, so he was thankful for the dark wrapping him round. He waited till the boy's back was turned, and then came skulking out from his hiding-place and without a word set off uphill along the familiar path at a great pace, with Mr. Swift and the nurse hurrying along behind him. This was the very track up which he had toiled on hot summer evenings carrying Kinza home from market; here was the fountain where he and Rahma had filled the buckets on dewy mornings at sunrise: to his left was the burying ground, with the three little graves where the marigolds grew, and there in front of him at the top of the hill gleamed the lights in the cottages on the outskirts of the village. Just another fifty yards' climb and he could see his own lamp-lit doorway and the rosy glow of the charcoal fire. He stopped short and beckoned his followers to his side. They were very much out of breath, for he was far more nimble than they were.

"There," he breathed, pointing towards it. "It is the

third house beyond the fig-tree. You just push the gate open—there is no latch. Don't be afraid of the dog—he's chained—and remember you have promised not to tell my father."

"Yes, Hamid," said the nurse quietly, "I've promised, and if your father comes with us to the car you must just hide till he goes away. We will not leave without you. Otherwise we'll meet you here."

They went cautiously on up the rocky path and Hamid went off to hide himself safely behind the bushes at the bottom of the burying ground. Crouching there, hugging his knees, he remembered his first escape, when he had crept down the hill at midnight and felt so afraid of evil spirits in the dark. Suddenly he realized that he was not afraid any more, and wondered why.

He soon remembered why. There was a hymn the English nurse had taught him, beginning "There is a beautiful Country." To those like himself whose hearts had been made white, death was no more a place of shadows and lost spirits—it was simply a door into the light and sunshine of God's Home, and the nurse had said that little children who had no knowledge of good and evil were welcome there, so probably his little brothers and sister were safe and sheltered and happy after all. Hamid suddenly wished he could go there, too, instead of crouching outside, an outcast within sight of his home. He yearned for the warm fireside, for the nuzzling goats, for Rahma, and, above all, for his mother. His heart strained towards her. Surely she would hear and come.

Mr. Swift and Rosemary reached the outskirts of the village, and by the light of a torch made their way single file along the mud track that led to Hamid's home. Nobody saw them passing, and when they reached the gate, it was as he had said. It opened with a gentle push, and they stepped out of the shadows and stood hesitating in the light that streamed through the open doorway.

There was the rattle of a chain and the big black dog leaped up and strained on his lead. The bearded man sitting just inside glanced out, saw them, and rose instantly and crossed the hut. There seemed to be a sort of scuffle inside, a quick murmur of low voices, and then the master of the house appeared, smiling and bowing and full of polite greetings. He begged his guests to enter and tell their business inside, and to partake of his meal even though the food was poor. Stooping, they passed through the low doorway and stood in the tiny dim room, looking round.

There was a young woman with a sad, patient face squatting by the fire and a shy little dark-eyed girl nestling against her. In a shadowed corner leaning against a bundled-up blanket sat an older woman. She did not come forward to greet them; she remained in her corner, silent and watchful, and the master of the house spread a sheepskin and bade his guests sit down with their backs to her.

Of Kinza there was no sign at all, and the nurse's heart sank—perhaps they had all come on a wild-goose chase.

Expressing polite surprise at the late hour of their visit, the black-bearded man told the young woman to serve them with sweet mint tea, and as they sipped he enquired of their errand.

"I have come to find out about your little blind girl, Kinza," replied the English nurse speaking very firmly. "She was left in my charge by her brother about seven months ago. I have grown very fond of the child, and would very much like to have her back. She is your child, and it must be as you wish, but I am willing to pay a price for her—and of course her mother can come and see her from time to time."

There was an instant's silence while the step-father,

completely taken by surprise by the assurance in her voice, hesitated. She had mentioned paying a price, and he would do almost anything for money; she would pay more than the beggar. On the other hand he might get into trouble for having taken her, and there was the question of her fine clothes. Kinza had arrived home after dark, wrapped in a potato sack, and had been kept out of sight ever since. He had sold her clothes to some Spaniards that very morning. It was too much to risk. He settled his face into a state of bewildered astonishment and spread out his hands, palm upwards.

"But I know nothing of the child," he assured her in an injured voice. "True, her brother stole her away some seven months ago, but since then I have neither seen her nor received news of her. If the boy has told you that this is her home, he is speaking the truth, but the child is not here, nor do I know of her whereabouts. If I hear news of her, I will gladly bring her to you."

There was a long pause. Rosemary's eyes met the eyes of the young woman sitting the other side of the fire. They were fixed on her very steadily and—was it imagination, or did she really give a very faint nod in the direction of the old woman?

Rosemary turned on her sheepskin and looked all round the room. There was only one possible place of concealment, and that was under the blanket behind the old woman. No longer caring anything about manners, she got up suddenly and stepped across the room, and called out Kinza's name at the top of her voice three times over.

The man stood on his feet, pale with fright; the old woman clutched at the rug, but she was too late. Kinza, who had been suddenly lifted from her mother's arms and dumped on a cold floor, was only sleeping very lightly. At the sound of the well-known, well-loved voice she sprang up with a loud answering cry. The old woman would have held her down, but her frantic struggles under the blanket betrayed her. Rosemary almost lifted the old woman out of the way, flung back the covering, and the next moment Kinza was in her arms, clinging to her as though she would never let go.

Kinza's joy was indescribable; all the terror was over and she was safe again in the strong arms of her protector. The last two-and-a-half days had been a sort of nightmare of jolting and cold as she had lain all night wrapped in a sack on the boards of a lorry-trailer; of cuffs when she cried, of hunger and fear and bewilderment, and of rough hands that snatched her from her mother's arms. But that was all over now; the voice she loved had called her to safety, and no one, she was certain, could ever pluck her out of that sure clasp. Her strained body relaxed and she lay at peace. Rosemary turned to face the step-father.

He had risen threateningly, his face pale with anger and fear, and Mr. Swift had risen too and stood ready to interpose. Mr. Swift was a big man, and Si Mohamed realized in a moment that his only hope now was to give in graciously and strike a good bargain. His expression changed almost instantly to forced amusement at Kinza's joy.

"There," he said laughing in rather a nervous way, "you have found her, and now she shall be your daughter. You are very welcome to her, and with you I know she will be safe and happy. Now what are you willing to pay for her? and she is yours!"

Rosemary, who had obtained all details from Hamid, mentioned a sum considerably higher than the beggar had offered. Si Mohamed, terrified that clothes were going to be mentioned and only anxious to get rid of his unwelcome guests, closed with the offer at once. He came forward to receive his price full of polite expressions of delight that Kinza should be so honoured. But Kinza, hearing the dreaded voice approaching, gave a little scream and, flinging her arms tight round Rosemary's neck, clung to her terrified.

Rosemary, handing over the money, stooped over the frightened child. "It's all right, Kinza," she whispered. "Don't be afraid. He can't touch you. You're my little girl now."

And Kinza, reassured and trustful, stuck two fingers into her mouth and lay still and content. She did not know that a long journey had been taken for her sake and that a high price had been paid to buy her back again, but the voice that had never yet told her a lie had said, "Don't be afraid; you're my little girl now." So Kinza was not afraid any longer. Right there in the presence of her enemy, resting in the arms of her friend, she fell asleep.

There was nothing left to do but to get away as quickly as possible before any further trouble arose. Rosemary said a brief goodbye to the old woman and the step-father and turned to speak to the mother, but her seat by the charcoal pot was empty. Only a little girl sat watching, solemn and big-eyed. The mother had slipped out unnoticed while the payment was being arranged, and, caring nothing for her husband's anger or the fact that her action would seem out of place, she was hurrying down the steep path that led from the village, stumbling in the darkness, calling softly and breathlessly to her son.

She guessed he must be near at hand, for how else could they have found the house? But even so she was startled when a little white-gowned figure, looking like a wraith in the moonlight, ran out from the shadows of the olives on the outskirts of the burying grounds and kissed her hand. She drew him fearfully back into the dark retreat of the trees and, crouching against a gnarled old trunk, she scanned his upturned face yearningly. "Little son, little son," she whispered, for she knew their time was short, "is it well with you? Is there no evil to you?"

"No evil to me!" he whispered back. "I work in the town and all is well—but Kinza—and my father—have they got her?"

His mother nodded. "The English woman paid a price for her and will take her as her daughter. I have no more fear for Kinza. All will be well for her and she will never suffer or be beaten or beg. But you, little son . . . come back to me. I miss you so."

He shook his head slowly. "I daren't," he breathed. "My father would kill me with beating. I have work and can live, and the English nurse feeds us at night. Besides, she has a Book about Jesus, the Man she told you about who took children in His arms, and in that Book is written the way of God which leads to Heaven. What she tells us from her Book makes my heart happy and I must know more."

He was speaking very earnestly and she drew him close against her. He had grown taller, but he was so thin, and to her he still seemed such a little boy; yet all on his own he had found a way of happiness. A moonbeam had struck through the silver leaves and she could see his face brighten as he spoke. If only she could follow him. She had no happiness.

"Then you must come and tell me, little son," she urged. "I want to be happy too. Your father won't beat you. He has to pay a boy to look after his goats, and he often grumbles because you are not here to work for him. He would be glad to see you back."

He rested his head against her shoulder and sat very still thinking hard. He was tired of travelling and wandering and fending for himself, tired of trying to be a man before his time. All he wanted was to be a little boy again, and to lean unashamed against his mother in the dark for a while and then to go home.

But if he did that, he would never learn to read from the nurse's Book and perhaps he would forget the way to Heaven. Besides, he was still very afraid of his father. Slowly, and after a long silence, he made up his mind.

"I will go back now," he whispered, "and I'll learn to read from the Book that tells the way to Heaven. Then when the harvest is ripe I'll come home and tell you all about it. Only ask my father not to beat me."

Steps sounded on the path and the light of a torch was flashed on to them. They rose quickly and came out into the open moonlight. The mother stooped and kissed her sleeping baby furtively, whispered a blessing on the nurse and gave her hand to her son. Then without another word she turned up the hill and went back to the punishment that awaited her, content and unafraid. Kinza was safe for ever, and she had seen her little boy. All was well with him and he had promised to come home. Nothing else mattered.

The little party hurried towards the valley. Mr. Swift had taken Kinza, and Rosemary held the torch; Hamid bounded ahead knowing every inch of the way. They had almost reached the car when they heard quick steps behind them and angry shouting. It was Si Mohamed, coming after his runaway boy. His wife's disappearance had roused his suspicions. The quiet joy in her face on her return had confirmed them.

"My father!" gasped Hamid and he made for the car like a hunted rabbit. Finding the door locked, he stood jumping up and down, squeaking with fear. The nurse was only a few seconds behind him, and the big English-man tossed Kinza into her arms as though she were a bundle of washing, jammed the key into the lock, dived into the front, trod on the starter, and opened the back. The nurse, Kinza, and Hamid all seemed to fall in at once as the car moved off with a triumphant roar. It shot past the empty market-place at thirty miles an hour, bumping horribly, leaving Si Mohamed standing alone with his shadow under the eucalyptus trees, very angry and out of breath, while his graceless step-son flung himself back against the shiny cushions and broke into a peal of laughter.

Five minutes later they had all settled themselves comfortably and got over their fright. Kinza slept deeply and peacefully, worn out by the terror and uncertainty of the past three days. Hamid rested his brown arms on the window, and his gaze wandered to the twin peaks above his home. He knew that he would come back, alone and on foot, one summer evening when the fields were ripe to harvest. And he would not feel very afraid, for Jesus had said, "I am the Light of the World: he that followeth Me shall not walk in darkness, but shall have the light of life."

19

WHILE Hamid sped off to adventure in the car, Jenny spent a long, long day at home. It was a day in which she had plenty of time to think, and while she was picking flowers, she tried to remember what Aunt Rosemary had said of a way out of a rather miserable life.

If only she knew more about the Lord Jesus, or if only she had a Bible and could read about Him! She thought rather vaguely of the picture in the Dispensary, and it reassured her. He was a Person so loving that children were not afraid of Him, and He wanted to come into her dark, closed heart, flooding it with light—comforting, forgiving, healing. And little by little, perhaps quite quickly, her cross, spoilt, vain little self would give way to the radiant Guest, and the strong, joyful, loving Presence within her would shine out, making her strong and joyful and loving too. "Like putting a candle inside an empty lantern so the beams shine out," Aunt Rosemary had said. She had specially remembered that bit.

"Please come, please come," she whispered, and lifted her face expectantly to the sun, one in spirit with the wide-open buttercups. Then she heard her mother's voice calling her, and got up and ran into her arms, her eyes starry bright with her new discovery.

"Darling Mummy!" she cried, hugging her, and then, suddenly shy, she went leaping off down the hill laughing and skipping over the rocks and waving her arms in the air as though carried away by some secret joy.

That night she had so much to think about that she was quite sure she would never go to sleep, and yet, when the light was turned out and she was left alone with the sound of the rushing stream in the valley, her eyes closed almost immediately, and the next thing she knew was that her mother was shaking her gently, and Auntie Rosemary was sitting at the foot of the bed laughing and holding a bundle wrapped up in the car-rug in her arms.

"It's Kinza!" cried Jenny, flinging herself on the bundle, and a tremendous hugging and kissing ensued. Kinza opened bright, drowsy eyes, but closed them again in a minute or two, and Jenny, very pink and warm with joy and deep sleep, nestled her head against her aunt's shoulder and heard all about it in a whisper; for after all it was two o'clock in the morning, and there were other guests in the hotel.

Everyone was hungry, so they lit the picnic primus and made tea. Mr. Swift, who was feeling enormously pleased at the success of the expedition, balanced himself on the bed-rail and stirred his sugar with a tooth-brush handle while his wife spread butter and honey on the bread and passed round the biscuits. Never had there been a happier midnight feast, and Jenny was going to remember that hour all her life. Kinza had been brought back, and all her naughtiness and its terrible consequences were forgiven and forgotten. She was going to start again, a new child in a new happy life and, sitting there in bed with all the people she loved best grouped round her, and her mouth full of bread and honey, she felt as full of happiness as the buttercups had been full of light. Her pure joy infected them all, and although her mother said rather weakly four times over that they really must all go to bed no one took the slightest notice; they just went on eating and whispering. When Mr. Swift told them how they had escaped from Si Mohamed, he fell backwards off the bed-rail in his excitement, and they all nearly burst with repressed laughter; whereupon Kinza woke, and sat up tousled and majestic, blinking at them solemnly like a baby owl. She apparently disapproved of all this midnight merriment, for after a few moments she cuddled back into the depths of the blanket and went to sleep again; then Mrs. Swift said for the fifth

time that they really must go to bed and Mr. Swift said,
" All right, but let me just have one more piece because
falling off the bed-rail made me hungry again," and then
Auntie Rosemary wanted another piece, and so did Jenny,
and her mother thought she might as well have one too.

Then Mrs. Swift said for the sixth time that they really
must go to bed, and this time they *did* listen to her. They
all kissed Jenny goodnight and tucked her up in turn, and
then went off down the passage laughing at Mr. Swift,
who was trying to walk quietly in his enormous squeaky
shoes, like an elephant trying to walk on tiptoe. And Jenny
was left alone with her happiness in the dark. God had
heard their prayers and Kinza had come back.

Everyone slept on next morning till the sun was high—
except Hamid and Aunt Rosemary. They got up at the
usual time, Hamid because he had slept excellently all
night on the back seat of Mr. Swift's car, and the English
nurse because she had a busy day ahead of her. It was still
quite early when she was disturbed by loud knocking, and
she got up with a little sigh, wishing she could train the
Moors once and for all not to come for 2.30 p.m. dispensary at 7.30 in the morning. But when she opened the
door she found only Hamid, his hands and face pink and
shining from a ducking under the fountain, come to visit
her.

His rags were dreadfully torn and dirty, and he had
nasty sores on his legs, but the child himself was as eager
and brimming with young life as the spring morning. He
kissed the nurse's hand, chuckled, and hopped uninvited
over the threshold. He seemed to have some particular
purpose in his visit, for he stood on one leg and scratched
his head for half a minute or so. Then, apparently not
feeling quite ready to come to the point, he enquired for
Kinza.

" She's all right," said the nurse. " Do you want to come
and see her?"

For an answer he skipped upstairs ahead of her to where

Kinza lay in her old corner on the mat, her dark head pillowed on her arm, fast asleep. Hamid nodded, well pleased, and then looked round hopefully to see if there was any prospect of something to eat. He had timed his visit perfectly, for the English nurse was just in the middle of her breakfast at the other end of the room. Hamid sat down cross-legged on the floor at a polite distance from the table, his eyes bright with expectation. He had not eaten honey sandwiches in the night, and he was very hungry.

The nurse gave him a bowl of sweet coffee and a big hunk of bread. He sipped it noisily, chuckling with pleasure between the mouthfuls. When he had finished and cleaned out the bowl with his finger for fear of wasting any sugar he drew a little nearer and said confidently, "Teach me to read."

The nurse looked at him doubtfully. "But so many people want to learn to read and they only keep it up about a fortnight. Then my time is all wasted."

He shook his head very emphatically. "I would go on every day, until harvest time," he said, "because then I am going home. My father will be glad to see me at harvest because he's so busy. Could I learn to read before harvest?"

"I should think so," said the nurse, "if you really come every day." Her mind ran over the busy hours and she wondered rather vaguely when she was going to fit in this new demand. But the child seemed very much in earnest.

"Why do you want to learn to read, Hamid?" she asked.

He lifted a sober brown face to hers and told her his simple little story.

"I want to go home," he said. "But if I go home and I can't read, who will go on teaching me the way to Heaven?"

"Then you believe it really is the way to Heaven?"

"Yes; I had a dream. I saw the Lord Jesus with His arms stretched out. I think He was on a cross. And behind the cross was a door, wide open, and He told me it was the way to God. And He told me I was to come to you because it was all written down in your Book."

"Very well," said the nurse quietly. "You can come every day just about now. We'll start at once."

She fetched her book of Arabic letters and found him a very quick pupil. By the end of half an hour he had learned quite a number of letters and was unusually pleased with himself.

"Aa—d—dd—rr—z," he chanted proudly. "Now I can read!"

He skipped off with his head held high, and the nurse went back with a happy heart to clear the breakfast things.

20

THE visit was drawing very near to its close now, and on the last Saturday they started off early in the morning and went for a picnic far up in the mountains—Mummy, Daddy, Aunt Rosemary, Jenny, Kinza and a fat picnic basket, all packed into the car together.

They drove up and up past clustered thatched villages and rocky slopes of heather; they looked down far below them into green gorges, and beyond rose mountains capped with snow. Still on and up sped the car until the road plunged into the cool shadow of pine-woods, where round the roots of the giant trees grew English primroses. They stopped the car, and Aunt Rosemary, who had not seen an English spring for ten years, was up the bank before Jenny, burying her face in the pale flowers.

Everyone fell silent and breathed deeply. Jenny flitted from clump to clump picking flowers, and having collected all she could hold she sat down on a stump in a patch of sunlight to arrange them.

And now she wanted to tell Aunt Rosemary her new secret. She must try to tell her today because there might not be another chance, but she did not know how to begin or how to say it, and she had not the slightest idea how to explain what had happened. Only she had felt quite sure something *had* happened and she must know what was going to happen next. Aunt Rosemary could tell her. "O God," she breathed into the sparkling air, "make Auntie come and talk to me here, so I can tell her!"

And God heard her prayer, for a few minutes later Aunt Rosemary wandered away from the others and came over to Jenny and sat down on the tree-stump beside her.

But although it was such a wonderful chance to tell her,

sitting there in the still forest, Jenny could find no words to begin. If only Aunt Rosemary would talk about it first, but Aunt Rosemary didn't; she was talking about English woods hundreds of miles away, dozens of years ago, and Jenny was not the least bit interested. There was only one thing that mattered now, and that was the great big thing that had happened to her two days before, and the more she tried to put it into words the more she found herself wondering what really had happened, and whether anything had happened at all. Perhaps it was all just a particularly bright pretend, and the joy would pass and the light would fade. Her eyes suddenly filled with tears of pent-up longing and then her mother called them to come and have dinner. The chance was gone and perhaps there would not be another one. God had apparently not heard her prayer.

She cheered up at dinner, because the high air had made her so hungry, and after dinner she and her father explored up-stream, which was great fun, but all the time there was the pain of disappointment deep down in her heart. Doubt had crept in, and all the light and happiness had gone.

They drove home in the golden evening, Jenny's head leaning against her father's shoulder, and the window wide open to let in the wind. It was a sweet warm wind, scented with arnica, and it made Jenny feel sleepy. She watched the flying landscape through half-closed eyes, until they came to a low water-meadow with white jonquils growing in clumps among the rushes. Then she suddenly remembered that the next day would be Easter Sunday, and she sat up rather quickly.

Jenny liked Easter Sunday. There were always white lilies and narcissi on the breakfast table, and big coloured Easter eggs round her plate. She always wore a new white frock and white ribbon in her hair. After breakfast she and her father and mother all went to church, which was unusual and exciting, and as far as Jenny could remember the park was always full of sunshine and bluebells and the orchard full of white blossom. The church too was arrayed in white—a beautiful riot of blossom, lilies of the valley, narcissi and golden daffodils—and the choir boys in white robes sang " Jesus Christ is risen today . . . Alleluia!"

Here they would not go to church because there wasn't one to go to, but suppose Jenny went to visit Auntie Rosemary early with white flowers—perhaps they could sort of play church together. And talking about churches might make Auntie Rosemary talk about God again, and then perhaps it would be easier to tell. She laid her hand on her father's arm. " Stop, Daddy," she said.

Mr. Swift stopped. "What's up?" he enquired good-naturedly.

"I want to get something," explained Jenny. She jumped out of the car and ran backwards a little so that Auntie Rosemary could not see what she was doing. She sped across the field, gathered an armful from the water's edge, wrapped them in her cardigan and sped back to the car. She tumbled in breathless.

"What have you got there, Jenny?" asked her father.

"A secret," replied Jenny. "We can go on now!" Mrs. Swift, who had been watching her nimble little daughter through the back window, smiled and said nothing. It was not till Jenny was tucked in bed and the narcissi were up to their necks in the water-jug that she understood what it was all about.

"Mummy," said Jenny, "it's Easter Sunday tomorrow, and on Easter Sunday there are always white flowers. Can I get up very early and take my narcissi to Aunt Rosemary as an Easter surprise?"

"Why, yes," answered her mother; "I think it would be lovely. She has been so kind to you, Jenny. You can go when you wake up. We won't wait breakfast, as you'll probably stay and have it with her. I'll put out your Sunday clothes now."

She laid out Jenny's best frock and clean white socks, kissed her goodnight and left her, and Jenny went to sleep at once, comforted and hopeful. Perhaps it was all going to come right after all.

She woke very early, when the watcher on the mosque cried out the dawn prayer-call, just at the time when in England the bells would start ringing to remind people that Jesus Christ had risen. Jenny lay for a time sniffing the narcissus-laden air, listening to the stream, and watching the silver advent light of sunrise brighten behind the wall of rock across the valley. Then she jumped out of bed, washed and dressed herself with extreme care because it was Easter, and set off.

She knocked at the door sedately, and Auntie Rosemary, who was up and having her breakfast, appeared at the window, surprised at such an early caller. Seeing who it was she ran down to open the door, and Jenny bounded joyfully in and held up her narcissi.

"White flowers for Easter!" she announced triumphantly. "I picked them yesterday without you seeing me."

They went upstairs hand in hand to where breakfast was laid on a white cloth, with a bowl of primroses in the middle of the table. They arranged the narcissi in a vase behind the primroses and sat down to enjoy themselves.

"It looks like a church at Easter-time, doesn't it?" remarked Jenny. As she spoke the sun rose behind the mountain and streamed into the room, blessing them with warmth and light. Jenny wriggled contentedly nearer to her aunt and helped herself uninvited to bread, butter, and jam.

"On Easter Sunday at home," she remarked when she was quite full, "Mummy and Daddy and I always go to church. It's a pity there isn't a church here, isn't it, so we could all go together?"

"Yes," answered her aunt, "I do miss going to church dreadfully, and yet you know, Jenny, it doesn't really matter in one way. The chief reason for going to church is to meet God, and we can meet God anywhere. I meet Him here every day in my room; just now when you came I was reading the Easter story and feeling so happy."

"Will you read it to me if you've finished eating?" asked Jenny eagerly, settling herself very comfortably to listen while Aunt Rosemary read about the woman who wept in the garden at dawn.

"He met Mary in a garden," said Aunt Rosemary; "and He met some of the disciples in a little room, and He met two others on the road, and He met Peter on the beach. So you see it isn't really necessary to go to a building."

"No," said Jenny simply, lifting a bright face; "that's what I wanted to tell you. The other day . . . the day you went to fetch Kinza . . . I thought He met me, up on the hill where the buttercups grow. I asked Jesus to come and live inside me like the light in the lantern, and stop me being cross and selfish. And I felt so happy and I thought He had come. But yesterday I didn't feel happy any more, and I was afraid perhaps it was all pretend. Do you think He really came, Auntie? because I don't really feel very different."

Aunt Rosemary was silent for a moment. Then she said quietly, "Jenny, how did Mary feel quite sure that Jesus had really come to her?"

"When He said her name," answered Jenny a little ruefully. "It was easy for her. She heard Him and saw Him."

"Yes, I know," said Aunt Rosemary, "but it's really quite easy for us too if only we believe that God speaks the truth. I'm going to show you a text, Jenny, and then I'm going to tell you a story."

"Good," said Jenny who loved stories; and she wriggled close to look over Auntie Rosemary's Bible. They read Isaiah, chapter 43 verse 1.

"For thus saith the Lord . . . Fear not: for I have redeemed thee, I have called thee by thy name; thou art Mine."

"That text reminds me of Kinza the night we went to look for her," said Aunt Rosemary glancing at the little hump in the corner that was Kinza asleep. "She was living with me quite happily, but she was stolen, and taken away from me. I love Kinza very much and I knew she'd be unhappy, so I went after her, and I found her hungry and frightened and wanting me. She didn't know I was there, but I knew she was there, so what did I do?"

"Shouted at her!" said Jenny with sparkling eyes. She knew this story well and would never tire of hearing it again.

Aunt Rosemary laughed. "Yes, that's right," she said. "But we'll put it a bit differently this time. Let's say I called her by her name. I said 'Kinza'—and what did Kinza do?"

"Bustled out from under her rug in no time," cried Jenny, and she too laughed delightedly.

"Yes, she bustled out in no time," repeated Aunt Rosemary. "She was unhappy and frightened and she knew if she came she would be safe and happy, so she didn't stop to ask how or why or if it was really me. She knew it was me by the way I called her by her name, and she came straight into my arms and felt perfectly safe; she knew she could trust her 'Ima', as she calls me. And that's exactly what happened to you on the hillside, Jenny. You didn't know much about Jesus; you were just miserable and tired of yourself. But Jesus knew all about you and He wanted to make you good and happy. So He called you by your name, and you knew it was He and you came at once and felt perfectly safe."

"Only for two days," answered Jenny cautiously.

"Yes, exactly," agreed Aunt Rosemary; "and that's just what happened to Kinza. She hadn't been in my arms two minutes before her step-father began talking, and Kinza began to tremble and cry. I was holding her just as close and loved her just as much, but as soon as she heard the voice of the man who had stolen her and beaten her she began to feel afraid and wonder if it was all right after all. And the minute we come to Jesus, Satan, our old master, who hates us to be good and happy, begins to talk very loudly in our hearts and tells us it's all pretend; and as long as we listen to him we shall feel afraid and worried. But our feelings don't really matter very much, because Jesus doesn't change. He holds us just as close and loves us just as much whether we worry about it. or whether we don't."

"Oh, I see," said Jenny thoughtfully. "I forgot about Satan."

"Well, you needn't think much about him yet," said Aunt Rosemary. "If you are really one with Jesus he can't touch you any more than that wicked man could take Kinza out of my arms. He can only frighten you if you listen to him. Now listen what happened next. I went up to Si Mohamed and I took the money out of my pocket and paid him, and if Kinza had been old enough to understand I'd have said this: 'Don't be afraid, Kinza. I've redeemed you—that means bought you back again. I called you to come to me and you came. No one can take you away from me now. You're my little girl for ever.'

"We really belonged to God, because He made us, but when we did wrong we wandered away from our real Master, and Satan said, 'They are mine now.' But Jesus loved us and wanted us back, and was willing to pay any price to redeem us, to buy us back again. The wages of sin is death, and Jesus was willing to pay even those wages because we were so precious to Him. He died on the Cross and paid the price, and now when He calls us and we come He says, 'Don't be afraid. I've paid for you. You'll never belong to anyone else now. You're Mine for ever!'

"I couldn't explain about the price to Kinza because she was too little and too sleepy, but I did just whisper, 'Don't be afraid, Kinza; you're my little girl now.' And Kinza did a very sensible thing. She believed me and she stopped being afraid. Although that cruel man was still standing in front of her talking, she just clung to me as close as she could and fell quietly asleep in my arms and slept all the way home. And the only way to stop feeling afraid is simply to believe what Jesus says. He died to pay the price of sin. He rose again on Easter Sunday so that He could live in the heart of every man and woman and boy and girl who hears His call and comes to Him; and if Satan says, 'It's not true; you're still mine,' just answer, 'Jesus says He's redeemed me; He's called me by my name; I'm His for ever; I believe Him and I'm not going to be afraid.' "

Jenny sat quite silent, thinking over what her aunt had said, and fingering the white narcissus petals. The sun streamed warm on her hair and she felt perfectly happy because now she understood what had really happened. Jesus had loved her and died for her and paid for her and called her and made her His own. All she had had to do was simply to come, and you couldn't go far wrong over that. All her life long from that moment onward Mary was going to be her favourite Bible character because they had so much in common. They had both got up early on Easter morning, and amidst sunshine and white flowers Jesus had called them by their names and taken away their fears and made them happy.

They talked for quite a while after that, and then Kinza woke up and wanted her breakfast, and Jenny went dancing off through the sunshine to find her father and mother. But Rosemary sat very still watching her curly-headed baby who sat with her face buried in her bowl of milk.

She had felt quite sure for the past few days that it was not safe for Kinza to remain with her any longer. As soon as the step-father wanted more money he could easily hire false witnesses and claim the child. For the next few years she must be taken somewhere out of his reach, and the obvious place was Jenny's Blind School.

And yet what Auntie Rosemary wanted more than anything else for Kinza was that she should be brought up by someone who would teach her to love the Saviour while she was still tiny, and that was why she had hesitated in accepting Mrs. Swift's kind offer. Now she knew the answer quite clearly. She would ask Jenny to teach Kinza, and pray that the Holy Spirit of God would teach Jenny.

21

When Jenny was finally told that Kinza was going home with them, she nearly went wild with joy and excitement, and danced about like a crazy little lamb. The thought of having Kinza to look after on the journey did much to lessen the sorrow of having to say goodbye to Aunt Rosemary; and after all it was not going to be a very long goodbye, as Aunt Rosemary was due home for a holiday in the summer, and had promised to come and stay with them all.

The evening before they left, Jenny took her aunt and Kinza for a last walk to the place where the buttercups grew, and they sat there together for a little while watching the sunset. .

"Are you sad that Kinza's going away, Auntie?" asked Jenny suddenly.

"Well, of course I shall miss her dreadfully, but I feel quite happy about her. You see, what I mind most of all for Kinza is that she shall learn to know and love the Lord Jesus while she's still tiny, and now that you know Him you'll be able to teach her. Of course, I expect she'll learn something at the Blind School, but such a wee child needs someone special all to herself to teach her."

Jenny looked very serious.

"I don't know an awful lot myself," she replied doubtfully; "who'll teach me, Auntie Rosemary? At school they don't talk like you do. We mostly learn the names of kings in Scripture. I suppose I could go to Sunday School, but we usually all go out in the car on Sunday afternoon."

"Yes, it does seem difficult," said Aunt Rosemary. "But it's quite all right, because you've got your Bible, and you've got the Holy Spirit of Jesus in your heart to show you what it means. There was a king called David long ago who wanted to understand the Bible, so he prayed this prayer: 'Open Thou mine eyes, that I may behold wondrous things out of Thy law.' God answered his prayer and whenever he read the Bible he saw all the way to Heaven mapped out in it; and he said this:

"'Thy Word is a lamp unto my feet, and a light unto my path.'

"If you read it faithfully and regularly every day, asking the Holy Spirit of Jesus to make you understand, you'll find that He lights up and explains all the things you find dark and difficult."

"There are such long words in it," said Jenny, still rather doubtful.

"Not in the gospels," answered Aunt Rosemary. "Start with those. And I'm sure you'll find Mummy and Daddy willing to explain hard words if you ask them. They are interested in everything that interests you. Have you told them what happened to you and why you want to read the Bible?"

"No," said Jenny frowning, "I wanted to, but somehow I couldn't explain."

"Well, it would be a very good thing to tell them in words," said Aunt Rosemary, "but a far more important thing is to tell them by works. If you have really put the Lord Jesus in the very middle of your life, if you obey His voice every day as He speaks to you in the Bible, He will soon change you very much. His love will begin to show instead of your selfishness, His patience instead of your bad temper, and His helpfulness instead of your laziness. And directly that begins to happen Mummy and Daddy will know all about it without any telling. But I should try to tell too, because it would be such a lovely thing to share."

"Yes," agreed Jenny frankly. "They'd certainly be pleased if I really got nice and good and never got into rages, and I expect they'd want to know why, too. I should think I'd better show them first, and then they'll believe me when I tell them. Let's go home now, and I'll show them I want to help with the packing." So they hurried home through the sunset as quickly as they could, Auntie Rosemary carrying Kinza in her arms, warm, heavy and drowsy.

Next morning at dawn they all gathered at the hotel door to say goodbye. Hamid appeared from some secret haunt of his own to see the last of his little sister. Mr. and Mrs. Swift were busy with porters and bills; and Aunt Rosemary, while she waited, stood watching the three children whom she had come to love more than any other children she knew. They stood in a little group by the luggage—beautiful, favoured Jenny; ragged Hamid; and blind Kinza. What widely-separated, lonely pathways lay ahead of them? Thank God there was a Shepherd who cared for lonely lambs, and a Light to guide their stumbling feet. And thank God there was a day coming soon when children of every kindred and tribe and nation would stand before the throne of God; and in that day they would all meet again: Jenny set free from herself, Hamid set free from his fear, and Kinza seeing the light—all would rejoice together.

A few moments later they had said goodbye and the car drove off toward the green valley. Jenny's eyes were full of tears, but Kinza, beating excitedly on the windows, had not yet realized that her dear "Ima" was not also inside, and when she did realize she would no doubt be quickly comforted with a biscuit. They swept round the corner, and Rosemary was comforted to find that one of her children, at least, was still close beside her. One great mission of Hamid's young life had been completely successful, but his little sister would never need him again. For her fine clothes, and big cars, and biscuits—for him the deserted market-place, the hunger, homelessness and rags.

"Come home and have breakfast," said the nurse at his side.

He brightened up instantly and forgot all his troubles—the thought of hot coffee and bread and butter turned all the world rosy. He raced along beside her, rubbing his hands delightedly. He had no work today because the master had gone to town, so there was plenty of time and, apart from this invitation, no prospect of anything to eat.

When breakfast was over he had his daily reading lesson. He was getting on very fast and the nurse marvelled at him. She had taught all types of children—the sheltered little girls from big houses, the wild waifs from the streets, and it was astonishing how much quicker the latter were at learning. Their wits and memories were sharpened by the struggle they had to keep alive, and they had trained themselves to look and remember. Hamid in a week had mastered all his letters and knew the repeating exercises by heart; in fact, he was rather unduly puffed up.

"Now I know everything," he remarked, beaming as he struggled through a few three-letter words.

"Oh, no, Hamid; you are only just beginning. You must practise and practise putting the letters into words, and you must come every day if you want to read the Word of God by harvest time."

He nodded confidently.

"By harvest time," he repeated. "Then I shall go back and read the Word of God to my mother. Then she will know the way to Heaven too, and when my step-father beats her and won't give her enough food, the Lord Jesus will make her heart happy."

"Will your step-father let you read the Word of God to her?"

"Oh, no; he says all books are bad but the Koran. But I shall read it in the granary when my mother is grinding corn and I shall read to my sister Rahma when we tend the goats on the mountain. My father will never know."

"But later on, Hamid, he will have to know, if you are going to follow Jesus faithfully. You will have to tell him and he may beat you. But Jesus suffered a great deal for you because He loved you. If you love Him, you must be willing to suffer a little, too."

He turned thoughtful, troubled eyes on her.

"I do love Him very much," he said wistfully, and rose to go, leaving his friend well content with the answer. He had not boasted, nor made any great profession. He had simply laid claim to the greatest power in the Universe— "I love Him," that lonely little boy facing his perilous future had said, and many waters cannot quench love, neither can the floods drown it.

It wasn't long before Hamid could read, he worked at it so persistently; and to Rosemary it seemed no time at all before she was bringing him his farewell meal of bread and lentils.

Hamid wasn't travelling alone; he had some companions. He had much farther to travel than the others, but packed in with the crusts and the water-bottle and the cherries he carried the staff of life and the bread of Heaven, and by night on the rough mountain roads his young feet would not stumble much nor stray far. For Jesus had said, "I am the Light of the world: he that followeth Me shall not walk in darkness, but shall have the Light of life."

She watched them as they scampered away, and at the end of the street they all turned round and waved, five gay little figures black against the sunset. Then they turned the corner, and the light seemed to swallow them up.

To the children who have read this book

Some of you sometimes write and ask me whether the stories I write for you are true.

This story is not altogether true; I have collected a lot of incidents from the lives of children I have known and woven them into the life of one child. Jenny is mostly made up, and the nurse might be one of any of the missionaries who work among children in Morocco.

But all the same the story has been written to give you a true picture of what can, and does, happen to children who live in a land where Jesus Christ is unknown. Without Christianity there is often very little kindness and mercy, and no hope of real joy. But if you think this is rather a sad book remember that by praying and taking an interest in those who have gone out to preach the Gospel, you can help to bring light and happiness to these children.

I live in the town to which Hamid brought Kinza, and I have stayed in his home village. I have known many little boys turned out homeless into the street because their mothers married again, and I have heard of unwanted babies left on doorsteps. I have seen blind children hired out to beggars, and known of others, happily adopted, who have been snatched back into lives of misery. I have also seen many who have travelled long weary miles in search of healing, and sometimes we missionaries have been able to help them.

On the other hand I have known men, women, and little children who were sad and sinful and afraid, and whose lives have been changed by the Gospel. All that Hamid said on the subject has been said to me by a homeless little boy who I believe has found real happiness because he heard about and accepted the Lord Jesus. There could be many more like him but there are so few missionaries to tell them.

So as you think of the town to which Hamid and Kinza travelled and of the long, long valley in which it lies, with its Eastern snow-capped Riff mountains and its hundreds of villages, will you sometimes pray for the children who live there?

Your friend,

PATRICIA ST. JOHN.